Back Home

Back Home

Emotional guide for NRIs who are on the fence about moving to India

Nupur Dave

ISBN 13: 978-81-948149-5-5
ISBN 10: 81-948149-5-2

Printed in India and published by BUUKS.

DEDICATION

To my sister, Rashmi.

CONTENTS

About The Author *13*

Acknowledgments *15*

Preface *19*

Prologue *23*

1. WHY NRIS MIGHT CONSIDER INDIA **30**

Introduction 31

Why You Should Move to India 33

India Makes You Brutally Prioritize 34

Every Day is New 36

India Heals 37

Loneliness in India May Be Less 41

India Might Better Your Relationship With Money 43

Logistical Support is Better in India 47

Risky Bets and the Humiliation of Being an Immigrant on a Visa 49

2. WHY NRIS MAY STAY BACK IN AMERICA **51**

When You Should Stay Back in America 52

Losing Status By Moving to India 53

Women Lose A Few Freedoms 55

Losing The Posh Life in India 56

Missing Out on the Outdoors 57

Social Circle Loss 59

Work Culture is Different 59

Education Loss 61

3. MYTHS AROUND INDIA 63

Myth 1: I Read the News About India So I Know India 64

Myth 2: People Steal 65

Myth 3: Tumse Na Ho Payega 66

Myth 4: India is A Third World Country and Is Conservative 67

4. LIVING IN DENIAL 69

A Confused Indian Might Live Like A Nomad 72

A Confused Indian Makes 'Eventually' A Safe Word 73

How to Get Out of Confusion and Denial: Getting Real 74

I Got Real and I Can't Move to India. Now What? 75

5. MOVING TO INDIA, A MISTAKE? 78

Consequences of Not Liking it in India 80

The Permanency of Moving 81

Do What is Right for You in This Phase of Your Life 82

Am I A Loser to Move to India? 84

Change Your Metric For Success 85

How to Position Your Move to Society 87

If I Move, What Is The Guarantee I Will Stay? 88

6. TYPES OF NRIS AND ADVICE FOR THEM **92**

Types of NRIs by Likes and Dislikes 93

You Do Not like India 93

You Like India, but Don't Really Want to Move 93

You Are Confused About Moving to India 94

You Are Not Confused and Want to Move 'Eventually' 94

You Have Decided to Move 95

Types of NRIs by Relationship Status 96

Singles 96

In a Dating Relationship 96

Couples 96

Families With Children 99

Financial Dependencies 101

Types of NRIs by Visa Status 102

Students 102

Recent Graduates 102

H-1B and Visa Issues 103

NRI on a Green Card 104

US Citizen 104

American-Born Confused Desis (ABCDs) 104

The Patriotic NRI 105

Who Says They Need Your Help in India? Maybe You Need Help 107

Is it a Fantasy? Judge Yourself by What You Do, Not What You Think 107

How to Actually Help India? 108

After Moving to India 108

Help While Visiting India 110

Helping From America 111

Other Activities You Could Do While Still Living Abroad 111

7. GETTING CLOSER TO A DECISION 113

How to Decide if India is for Me 114

Compilation: Steps to Decide 114

How to not Decide 118

Do You Fit in? 118

Fear of Missing America is Not a Good Way to Eliminate India 120

Do You Really Need India or Do You Just Need a Break? 122

Your Annual Visit Might Be Deceptive 124

Deciding Through the Eyes of Friends 128

Your Friends Won't Give You the Right Reason 130

Gut Feeling: is India for Me Right Now? 131

Justifying Your Own Non-Action 132

This Is a Hard Decision 133

8. WHEN WILL YOU MOVE? THE TIPPING POINT 135

Salary Gets in the Way of Moving 141

Unrealistic Expectations of What India is Like 143

Finding a Job in India 144

9. ADJUSTING IN INDIA **148**

Introduction to Adjusting in India 149

Accept Things That Won't Change 150

ADOPT and ADJUST: Take up Local Rules 152

Adjusting to the 'You Have to Know' Culture 153

Adjusting by Not Looking for America in India 156

Adjust to a Judgmental Society 157

The Cost of Settling Down 158

Quality of Life in India Depends on Micro Location 160

Stay With Family or Not? 161

10. THE OFFICE **164**

Your Temperament Decides How You Accept Work Culture 165

What Is Really Different in Indian Work Culture? 166

- Working in India Is Great Fun 166
- Indians Are Emotional 168
- NRIs Seen As Privileged 170
- Punctuality is an Issue 171
- Unprofessional and Immature 173
- 'Everyone is Not Your Peer' Culture 174

Women at the Workplace 175

Will You not Move Out of Fear? 176

Dealing With the Change 177

- Change is so Large You Won't Notice the Small 178

Choose Better Work Content 179

Being Around Family 179

Be in a Position of Power 180

Don't Jump Right Into the Culture 180

What If You Are the Bad Culture? 182

11. THE CONCLUSION 184

What to Do in Your Last Few Days in America 185

Write Your Own Chapter 186

Appendix 189

Exercise 1 - The Fear 189

Exercise 2 - Missing America 189

Exercise 3 - Take the Juice Out of America 191

ABOUT THE AUTHOR

Born in Pune (India), Nupur Dave is an engineer who worked at Google for 10 years in the USA. After 13 years abroad, she moved back to India in 2016 and has published two books so far. She has worked with the Prime Minister's Office, is one of 12 in India to be awarded the LinkedIn Spotlight Award (2019), and was the COO of the Indian Googler Network. In her free time, she enjoys writing, food photography, and sports (She founded the Google Women's Cricket Team and has run a full marathon). She currently offers consulting services to NRIs on moving back to India. You can find her at www.nupurdave.in, on LinkedIn at Linkedin.com/in/nupurdave/, or Instagram and Twitter as @nupurdaveauthor

ACKNOWLEDGMENTS

Writing a book is one of the most stressful things I've done. I've bounced off my bed at 2 AM in mid-sleep to scribble sentences in the darkness of my room, only to be unable to decipher them the next morning. I've walked up and down my hall, reading pages aloud. My room's walls were decorated with misaligned post-it notes, reshuffled so many times that their stickiness wore off, and many dropped to the floor each time the fan was turned on.

Even training for a full marathon wasn't as stressful as writing a book! Hard work isn't the problem – creating something from nothing is. It is intimidating. I'd compare endlessly: "Look at how Stephen King wrote this paragraph! How will I ever invent such gems?" It is self-doubting: I mean, why will anyone want to read me? And it adds pressure for perfection: This paragraph is not good enough. It's got to be made better!

I didn't come out of self-doubt alone. On days where I had a conflict, I would call up my sister and ask something like 'This sentence about Chintu is making me sound very judgmental; what should I do?' While her kids were jumping on her trying to snatch the phone to talk to Nupur Maasi, she would quickly resolve it for me with an 'It sounds okay. Just leave the last part out.' While I was tapping endlessly at the keyboard with my headphones on, listening to anything from 21 Brahmins to Ariana Grande remixes, my mother would say, "Computer *par su karti reh che aa chokri*?

(What does this girl do at her computer the whole day?)" Yet, she was always selflessly cooking food for me.

I've been meaning to write a book for 10 years. I found inspiration in the oddest of places. While I was with Google, California, someone I didn't know yet found my office desk, after wandering about my floor asking for me, and told me: "I've read your blog. You should write a book." My sister, Rashmi, encouraged me to enroll in creative writing classes while I was still working at Google. I am extremely thankful to Google for the opportunities it gave me to pursue my interests.

I must thank my friends through college. Rahul Srinivas, who has not stopped pulling my leg since college days; Sai and Saket Jamkar, BVHK, Ani Basu and Amit Bhargava – you folks are awesome. Bhavna Kapoor and Vinayak Nagpal, I've known you for more than half my life, and I am blessed to have friends like you both. Can't wait to visit you at your warm Berkeley home, take Apu for long walks, and go to that torturous barre class again.

I must also mention Aditi Shrivastava, my writing buddy! My fond memories of America are about weekends in Berkeley with her. We'd put the timer on and quietly tap away at our laptops. Aditi, thank you for motivating me to write and keeping me awake with your awesome masala chai.

Daria Smerd, you've been my rock-solid friend for more than a decade! I am so lucky to know you! Karthika Periyathambi, I hope to prank you back one day! Arun Simha, thanks for gifting me that book and the bunny chow at One Embarcadero. Bharat Jayakumar, thanks for reading my first book and being always approachable. A big shoutout to all my friends from the Bay Area Quiz Club (BAQC), Google and from other offices for being ever excited for me and encouraging me – you know who you are.

A huge thank you to my extended family for being happy and excited for me all the time. To those whose experiences I have included in this book, I am touched that you came forward and opened up to me. Your experiences will help all the readers of this book. Thank you so much!

My fuel is my family. To Mom, who is always wondering what I am up to; Dad, who is always correcting what I am up to; Rashmi, who is always happy and always picking up my calls even if to say, "I'm in a meeting!"; Tushar, my brother-in-law who is always solving my problems in a jiffy; Rushat, my nephew who is growing up to be our family's anchor and my next advisor; Smera, my niece and best friend; Aai, who always offers unparalleled support and enthusiasm; Baba, who represents all things sports, Sanskrit and *sanskriti*; (Late) Dadi, whom I dearly love and miss; (Late) Dada, who will always be an army man: *"Bharat Mata ki raksha kaun karega?"*; and (Late) Aaji, who always had infinite encouragement for me – thanks for helping me become *more* me and supporting me in pursuing my interests.

PREFACE

In 2017, I was in Bangalore, a ten-month-old returnee from America, and I decided to pen down my reasons to move to India. I wrote a blog post for my friends, like I always do, and posted it without thinking much, like I always do. In a matter of two hours, my phone was overrun with the continuous sounds of *ping, ping, ping*. The post went viral. Thousands of NRIs reached out to me. It so happened that the feelings I expressed as an NRI – of lonely lives and missing my motherland – were the feelings of millions of immigrants, not just Indians.

I have various topics I want to write books on. However, there are many NRIs dizzy with doubt, which makes the topic of moving to India impactful and the need immediate.

That's how this book was born.

But wait! Still, I didn't want to write this book. I was terrified. *What if my circumstances change and I HAVE to or WANT to move back to America? How embarrassing and hypocritical I will look! Will NRIs throw eggs on me when I walk on the streets of New York? Will I get 'Bitch please!' emails in my inbox on Friday nights? Will I be tagged by the Re-Returned NRI Condemnation Society on Facebook? Will people throw their heads back in laughter at parties and spill wine on my dress and call me a loser?*

I told myself, "So what? I am but a medium." I wish there had been someone who could have guided me while I was in the US about how and where I should live my life. I know there are thousands of NRIs who need guidance. If my experience can be of some help to them or help pacify them, I will consider this to be the greatest impact of my life.

If you're an NRI looking for the answer to 'Which electrical adapter should I buy when I move to India?' you could use this book to prop up that bulky adapter against the wall. But if you're an NRI looking for answers to 'Will I like it if I move to India?' you should grip this book firmly in your hands and keep it by your nightstand, within close reach.

The goal of this book is to

1. calm the NRI's emotional doubts and fears,
2. guide the NRI on how to and how not to make the decision to move to India,
3. give the NRI a view of the other side.

Read all parts of this book if you want practical, emotional guidance about moving to India. Read it even if you *don't* want to move to India.

This book can be used by Indian diaspora living anywhere, though I have specifically addressed the USA – loosely called America or the US throughout the book – for two reasons:

1. I lived in America for 13 years, and I am most familiar with life there.
2. America has a high percentage of white-collar Indian diaspora. One would expect this book to be more relatable to a software engineer bothered by java errors rather than to a carpenter in Kuwait.

The statistics, facts, and immigration/visa rules mentioned in this book are true at the time of writing the book. I have leaned on the experiences of several NRIs to bring to life the points I am explaining. Wherever the person concerned was comfortable with their real name being mentioned in the book, I have done so. As for the rest, I have changed their names to alliterative names while retaining their thoughts and experiences.

If you see any bias in this book, it's but obvious – I am a mortal with experiences and preferences and, hence, opinions. I am sure you might shrug your shoulders and shake your head on reading a line or two in these pages. I would perhaps be glad if this happened, for to agree on everything would make even sugar too sweet!

What can you do for me? Enjoy the book. Then buy five copies for your crowded shelf and gift them to your friends. Add a review on Amazon and post it on your Facebook wall. Spread the love!

PROLOGUE

MY LIFE IN THE USA

Throughout my life, I did what other *desis* did. I rote-learned chapters of my school books, filled up a poorly designed form to enroll in an engineering college, and stressed over the GRE exam. Then I flew abroad for a master's degree, in a subject that I really didn't know much about, and looked around for a job to recover the money I'd spent. I never thought about returning to India. It wasn't a question that came to my mind.

Everyone has an aunt in America. I do too. When I decided to go to America, my father called up my aunt.

"HAYLO? HAYLOWWW!!" shouted my dad into the phone at our Pune house. Dad treated international calls as if they were emergency plane landings in his backyard. "*KEM CHO?!*" shouted Dad into the phone, "Nupur got admission in Georgia Tech."

"She must stay with us for a few days!" said my aunt.

And I was set. I had an education to pursue, a home to orient myself in, and an aunt to dote on me. What could possibly go wrong?

I'll be honest. I hated America when I got there. The moment I stepped out of the flight, I felt alien and poor. I had no freedom to move without a car and no money to buy even *chai* (tea). In fact, there was no chai to buy. The chai latte that Starbucks serves is as far away from chai as chai can be.

Everything in America is upside down. The cars drive on the right, the light switches are pushed up to be ON, and Coke is cheaper than water. Friends treat you on your birthday instead of you treating them, the winters are icy, and the summers are surprisingly hot.

I had classic rookie reactions in my first few months in America. The toilet stalls had gaps in them, and it made me conscious enough to hurry. I responded honestly to the saleswomen at malls who asked the don't-bother-to-reply-question 'Hey, how you doin' today?' I had accent understanding issues and struggled to decipher sentences like 'You gonna pay-bah kesh awe creddi?' Every morning, I would discover something new – the wrong type of football on TV or the wrong way to dress for the suddenly chilly weather as I wasn't in the habit of checking the weather every single day.

I had no money and earned my rent dishwashing in the university food courts. I sat through classes hungry or ate cereal thrice a day. Like other international students, I too had no parents backing my flight tickets for an I-miss-my-daddy moment. Because I was poor in the US, my focus had shifted from the real reason of education that I'd come to America for, to pure survival. *What am I going to eat, how can I save money,* and *I miss my mom* were top of mind every day.

One weekend, I waited an hour in the cold winter for a university bus that never came. I discovered it was daylight savings time, which meant the clock was offset – I was a whole hour early for the bus. I cried. I hated it all – The wait, the classes, the no-food, the no money, the cold chipping through my clothes and biting my bones. I wanted to leave America right then.

Five years later, I was still in America.

Life was much better. I was earning. I was employed with Google, the #1 place to work for at that time. There were so many promises for a great future. I was traveling internationally for work. I visited Sydney and Dublin multiple times. I transitioned to expensive $45 shampoos, visited high-end salons to cut my hair, and bought my clothes from Nordstrom. I was super fit as I was working out every day, and I had professional trainers, running buddies, and boot camp buddies. I had access to the best of anything in the world. And I always maintained that I wanted to eventually move back to India. However, there wasn't any urgent reason to leave that life.

Despite being blessed with opportunities, I was stressed all the time – Stressed about food and grades as a student, stressed about saving money and finding a better job as a young professional, stressed about finding a husband, stressed about which friends to meet on weekends, stressed over looking good and gym visits, stressed that I had to drive to get anywhere, stressed over parking, stressed over a lack of guidance and stressed because I was tired all the time due to my hobbies.

I missed not only my family, but I also missed India. There was an ease of life in India that I yearned for because my American life was so stressful. There was also a bit of guilt bubbling up in me. I felt bad I was spending money on luxury, while many people in India were struggling to even eat. By my 12th year in the US, it became ridiculous to live this way – my body in America but my mind in India.

Coming back every day to an empty home over 10+ years really affected my ability to tackle issues in my career. Home itself felt like a battlefield to me. I must admit I found it challenging to consider marriage to men who wanted to live in America. I knew I wanted to move back, so I would hesitate to date anyone too rooted in America. And I tell you, a helluva lot of Indians I met were! Now, I sometimes look back at that resolution and evaluate it. *If I had got married and settled in America, would my feelings to move back to India have changed?* The answer I've validated is no! I would have been distracted for the first couple of years of marriage, but once settled in, the feeling of trying out India would have returned and haunted me.

After 10–12 years of fearing my future, I realized the shocking truth that my stress wasn't going away unless I changed something big. I had tried everything by then – changing jobs, locations, friends, homes. The stress had merely disappeared from one area of life only to resurface in another area. I got physically and mentally exhausted. I decided that moving to India was going to be the change that would help me.

It was hard to leave Google, but it was harder to leave America. Leaving Google was scary, but I could return; it wasn't changing the quality of my life. But leaving America was about letting go of unknown opportunities. *What if I was to find a husband in the USA? What if my salary increased? How will I manage vacations in Europe?*

I came to a tipping point where the weight of these unknown future opportunities became less than the desire to explore my country so that I could live a better life, without stress. And it proved to be the medicine I needed. Some of the stress melted away immediately, the part concerning money and logistical support. The stress of fitness and my job took some time to go away. Eventually, I was able to experiment and find what I really wanted to do, and who I wanted to be.

My biggest realization? I realized how poorly I was approaching life in America. I was doing it all wrong by obsessing over the gym, my friends, dating, money, my job, and everything else. There were too many self-imposed constraints, too much peer pressure, too much of living cautiously. Maybe I am being too harsh on myself, but looking back, I feel I could have done my American life better.

Living with family and experiencing India as an adult has helped me handle life better. I'm ready to take on the challenge: Give me America now, and see how differently I take to it! If I ever move back to America, I know I will do things differently. I would spend money on convenience and make fewer acquaintances. Yes, I had too many acquaintances! I'd spend more money on learning skills and travel more.

I don't know if I will go back to America. I do miss it a lot! But at this point, while writing this book, I feel I have moved on, and I have a lot to explore here in India. I want to visit the majestic mountains in the north, the grand temples in the south, and lay down in the grass with the monsoons showers on my face.

As far as you are concerned, your journey is very unique, and you may or may not relate to what I've written. Do take whatever you feel is relevant to you. I hope my experience, fears, and thoughts in this book can help you with your decisions. Thank you, dear readers!

दुर्लभं भारते जन्म[1]

1 "It's a rare privilege to be born in India." Source: It's a modification of a phrases rooted in Adi Shankaracharya's *Vivekacūḍāmaṇi*. Though I couldn't find the quote verbatim in the text, I first saw this phrase on a t-shirt once and have been in love with it ever since.

1

WHY NRIs MIGHT CONSIDER INDIA

Introduction

We all knew Pankaj Pandey was never going to move back to India, but he was in denial in every form of his existence and praised India as if it were his wife. Once, during a chatty lunch at a *chaat* restaurant in Sunnyvale, he told me a secret.

"Nupur, I am going to visit India next week. To find a girl for marriage," he said while chewing a mouthful of vegetarian biryani, some rice flying out of his mouth.

"But I thought you wanted to move to India for good?" I asked, raising my eyebrows.

"No, no, not now. In a couple of years," he said, adding more biryani to his plate.

"What if you get married and your wife doesn't want to move back?" I asked, while chewing on the flavored rice.

"So I thought about that. I'm going to find a girl who will want to marry me, be willing to move to America, and then will want to move back to India," he predicted.

"Whaaaat?" I gulped my food. "What if she changes her mind here?" I questioned, though I had to admit I admired his conviction.

That was seven years ago. Since then, Pankaj has bought a three-bedroom house in San Jose and has his second child on its way. He's dropped all talk of moving to India.

According to the Ministry of External Affairs, India, there are 13+ million Non-Resident Indians (NRIs) living in the world as of 2019. Nearly 1.2 million of these NRIs are in America. Roughly 80% of them, at some point in their foreign lives, have thought about moving back to India. Yet, very few move. There isn't much data available to understand how many have moved back. A LinkedIn search for my 1st degree connections with foreign university degrees shows about 5-10% of these NRIs are back in India – indicating there's a magnitude of difference in this directional flow of Indians.

There seems to be a moral code around moving to India, as if it is every NRI's responsibility to move back. They call it the #reversebraindrain and I disagree with this statement. Because it sounds as if all brains are outside India and Indians living in India are stupid – as if we need NRIs to return and raise the average intelligence! You, as an NRI, should move to India only if you think it is the right thing to do at this phase of your life.

A tiny part of returned NRIs make a disruptive 'reverse brain drain' sort of impact, and though I really hope you're one of them, perhaps we should not assign moral codes to this. It makes NRIs sound like a cult. It also raises expectations for NRIs. They innocently expect to get the best jobs, expect to move up in line to be picked for these jobs, and expect the highest salary offers. It's best for NRIs to evaluate themselves and their own lives, instead of measuring themselves with a moral code and finding solace in the false notion that this is #reversebraindrain.

You, as an NRI, should move to India only if you think it is the right thing to do at this phase of your life.

NRIs have multiple reasons to *not move*. We will examine these reasons to understand why you shouldn't move before we discuss why you should move. Then we will talk about the fears NRIs face. Fear of the future, society, salary, and adjusting-ability are a few reasons in this non-exhaustive list of worries. Understanding your worries will help settle the dust on the muddy battlefield –

the battlefield of our struggle to live life more meaningfully. We'll address those fears and handwrite some solutions on the blank, though yet confusing, sheets staring at us.

Why You Should Move to India

I am firm on this advice as a default – Don't move back to India.

Yes, you read it right. *Don't move.*

Did you think I am going to sell the idea of India? Nope! I am *not* going to say 'You *must* come to India. It's so much better.' The default advice, in fact, is that when confused, don't move.

India is a fantasy for many. The NRI thinks he wants to move, but he doesn't actually want to move. He loves his American life, yet sometimes he fantasizes about the life he might have in India. He might get to lead a team of 200 people like his college friend does. He frowns at his US salary and wonders how life would be if he can get an expat's US salary in India, just like his India vice president (VP) does. He treks on weekends but visualizes road trips to the Himalayas, like he's seen in the Instagram photos of his younger cousin. The NRI might be mildly unhappy with his life and want the seemingly best part of someone else's life. Dear reader, be aware. Is the lack of excitement in your life pushing itself as a reason for you to move?

NRIs have some expectation of India being an elixir. Though I would agree it worked on me, giving me a high dose of happiness and healing that I badly needed in my life. Will it work for you? We don't know. Read on to see how you feel.

Always remember that when you're confused, don't move!

In this chapter, we will discuss the advantages and disadvantages of moving and some myths concerning India. Remember that these experiences of India are non-transferable. Only you can decide how you feel. But there are some serious reasons why India could work out for you, and I want to share them with you.

India Makes You Brutally Prioritize

In India, we face what is called *roz ka kich kich*, which translates into small but irritating everyday problems. This means, to live optimally in India, you have to choose what to get upset about – India makes you brutally prioritize. Otherwise, you could be on edge all the time, in the process, messing up your mind and life totally.

This *roz ka kich kich* is absent in America. You do have problems in America, often jokingly called first-world problems. The entry ramp traffic on Peachtree Blvd takes you 15 minutes to the office, and that makes you feel like the traffic is terrible, a comment you make to no one in particular when you keep your bag on your work desk. The Bollywood dance class is at the other end of the office campus, and you will be six minutes late. There was a Sonu Nigam musical show at 7 PM, and your friend canceled on you. This is a first-world life, and it becomes routine. Normal becomes boring. The first-world life is not appreciated anymore, for humans will always find new things to complain about. No matter how great America is, everyone in America will find something to complain about.

The *roz ka kich kich* is present in India, and it changes life completely. No longer are you experiencing first-world problems. These are real problems. My Delhi experience went like this: *Yesterday, there was no water in the overhead tank. Today, the electricity is out, but only in my room. The taxi I waited for canceled. Two older neighbors fought over parking space. There is a rat in my office. The cleaning lady hasn't taken out the trash for three days, the fruit vendor hid two bad apples amidst better apples, and the parlor lady didn't give me the discount she promised.*

What should I get pissed off with today?

I have to pick what to react to. I have to conserve my energy by brutally prioritizing my problems.

Roz ka kich kich is not visible to NRIs or visitors to India. Therefore, NRIs can't understand why resident Indians don't shush loud noise-makers in the cinema halls. They don't understand why no one stops people from walking on the road instead of the sidewalk and why no one protests against ladies who are skipping the restroom line. NRIs can't get why Indians don't stand up for what they see is wrong. And all this while, Indians are dynamically choosing where to spend their energy.

Where are we going with this?

In India, there will be a glaring number of *roz ka kich kich* problems. You have to brutally prioritize, filter, and choose your own happiness. America has no real (logistical) problems, so the human mind focuses on the next most potent problem it can see – Like the on-ramp, bumper-to-bumper traffic at 5 PM, the Indian store being too far, or roommates that drank your orange juice.

The thing with many cultures, not just India's, is that one interaction can mess your mind. My Polish friend, Daria Smerd, who is a manager at Google, Dublin, once told me, "In Poland or some EU countries, you walk into a place to buy bread, and that might just ruin your day. Residents are very direct, often tired or frustrated (because they are exploited and underpaid), or simply unhappy. They express their frustration by projecting on others or snapping at them." It is not uncommon in many countries to face some version of *roz ka kich kich.*

When you have to brutally prioritize your problems, it strips you off things that don't really matter. What remains is only and only what seriously means something to you. Living in India, you learn to pick your battles. It helps you discover yourself. This is one of the reasons I like India. India has problems, and perhaps we should celebrate it, for it keeps us grounded and keeps us real.

When you have to brutally prioritize your problems, it strips you off things that don't really matter. What remains is only and only what seriously means something to you.

Every Day Is New

There is a section of the NRI community, including couples, that has moved to India to get rid of the monotony and boredom they faced in America. They complain that every day felt the same – same route to office, unchanging desk, mechanical route home, closed neighbors' doors, no humans in sight, and weekdays dedicated solely to work, leaving only weekends to do things you like. It's called 'living from weekend to weekend,' and it is not exciting unless you take good care to fix it.

On the contrary, in India, there is so much going on that every day is new. India is full of surprises.

My parents' home, like a million homes in India, has human traffic starting at 6 AM – the watchman, the milkman, the maid, and the newspaper guy ring the bell. The maid greets me every day when I roll off my couch to make way for her dusting. Sometime in the day, the iron guy and the garbage guy come in to collect their regular loads. A vegetable seller pushing her cart outside shouts in a shrill voice, "*bhaaaji-yaaaaannn!* (vegetables)" while the road sweeper brushes the sidewalk and a putt-putting rickshaw stops to offload its passenger. There may not be time to get bored. There is so much noise here, a far reach from when I'd switch on a noisy space-fan in America just to hear some noise while I slept. Every day in India is new and happening, and monotony can't force itself to be part of India, ever.

It is but obvious that different people take to locations differently. You must explore to find what works for you before you make your decision. However, there are some areas where India definitely trumps America by magnitudes. This difference is a universal truth. Let's look at aspects of India that *will* work for everyone.

India Heals

It took me 12 months to get over him.

When I first met him on a date our parents had arranged for us, I fell in love. My feelings were probably accelerated because of his soft voice and handsome features. I felt lucky and relieved that I'd finally found someone and that I was finally going to get married at this *old* age of 29. The hall was booked; the wedding cards were printed. I dreamed of the wedding and the red sari I would wear – *No, no, maybe I'll wear a panetar and then change into a pink ghagra.* I dreamed of where I would live after marriage, San Ramon or San Francisco? While I was dreaming, I missed the signs that said *he's not that into you.*

It was a Saturday afternoon in San Francisco, on a patchy grass blessed by the California sun, where he said, "I don't want to marry you." I didn't realize how fast I got up, walked to my car, shut the door, and wailed loudly in the emptiness of my vehicle. The pain of the words and the shattering of my wedding dreams were too much to bear. I fell into deep, deep sadness.

As an immigrant with no family around me in California, I had to deal with my broken emotions on my own. The physical distance from my family in India also distanced them from the realities of a bad relationship. They couldn't register in their mind the gravity of what was happening in my life in America. I was unable to get the support I needed.

For months, I looked lost in the office. I couldn't sustain the smiles that my face previously carried. I would constantly eye the digital clock, waiting for it to flash 5 PM, so that I could drive to a home I didn't want to see – dark, suffocating, and lonely. In those winter evenings, my pain would numb me; all I could do was lay in bed and stare at the ceiling. Time would fly. 5 PM would become 8 PM, and my pillow would be wet from the tears that flowed like a steady river from the lakes of sadness that my eyes had become. I'd waste my time on Netflix, spend money on clothes I couldn't afford, and wake at three in the morning, crying till I couldn't breathe. At work, triggered by a memory, I'd run from my desk to hide in the ladies' room, unable to hold my tears. I didn't know what was happening to me.

What I needed was the unconditional love of my family, but I had only a few caring friends to help. With worry lines on my forehead, I'd tell them over lunches I didn't feel like eating, "I don't even know how to console myself." There were many people to help me through this, and yet, there was no one to help me through it. My family support happened immigrant style – only on the phone and only twice a day. 5:30 PM PST, when my mother woke up, and 9:00 PM PST, when my sister reached office, the only place she was undisturbed by her small baby crawling into her lap.

It was difficult to continue seeking help from friends. I'd think aloud, "It's been four months. I can't possibly tell them I'm *still* feeling lifeless and pathetic."

There was a missing of support from society – the culture that doesn't judge you also minds its own business. Colleagues who knew about my situation didn't say anything. 'See a counselor' was an answer I'd get from anonymous mailing lists. The answer irritated me. *See a counselor? For one hour a week? That's not enough time!* The lack of empathy from my office and the lack of family, society, and local support made my healing slow and painful. It took me a long and unbearable 12 months to get back on my feet.

But in India, the landscape of heartbreak was completely different.

My heart broke again in India. He was a good man, but again, destiny didn't mean him for me. After we decided 'This is not going to work, so let's break it off,' I sat on the kitchen floor and cried, my legs folded into my body and my chin propped on my knees. My mother, making roti's on a gas flame, looked at me askance and said, "Move on now. The chapter is closed." I cried even more. I cried the next day and the days after that.

My family was there to help me, in person, every single time. On random mornings, I would walk to Dad – my eyes red and tears wetting my cheeks – and my rational father would say, "Ohh *beta*, why must you cry? You must celebrate. Come, let's eat mango ice cream." I would ask in insecure moments, "Mummy, am I a bad person?" "Of course not!" she would say, giving me the unconditional love that I needed.

Office life in India helped too. People noticed and did something about it, "You're so quiet, Nupur. Is everything okay?" The mature empathized and the younger ones said silly things to make me feel better. They took me for walks, distracted me. They didn't ask questions; they told me what I wanted to hear. The same office people that would irritate me by not minding their own business helped me with the empathy that I needed. The pain was soothed, faster than anything I'd experienced in America. It felt like I was on a booster dose of healing.

India turned out to be a healing destination for me. I felt better able to handle my personal problems with family around. It makes me wonder if immigrants have more battles to fight on foreign lands. For instance, could you, an NRI, have a better career progression if you had family around you?

There is another healing that India offers – to the whole world – which is the healing of a spiritual kind. Indian Vedic philosophy, its science, and its way of life are an attraction for people of all colors. It has made India a healing destination for the world. The Beatles, Steve Jobs, and Mark Zuckerberg are some of the noted personalities who visited Indian ashrams. Thousands of unknown people come to India to live and learn about *Sanatan* dharma. A trek on the side of a chilly Himachal stream and eating a roadside vendor's spicy moong can cure you of any mental baggage you have. Life here is raw – and raw life is grounding. And in grounding, you find yourself and your inner voice.

Another reason I find India healing is the contrast in how American and Indian cultures approach small problems. In America, no problem is small, and everyone gets help when needed. However, this also means that any little problem is an escalation in America.

Sprained ankle? Go to emergency care!

Did someone touch your freshly cut hair in jest? Report to HR at once!

Someone asked where you're from? How dare they!

This makes you start taking yourself too seriously.

India is different for two reasons. First, there are lots of small problems, and you have to learn to let go. What would you do if your teammates touch your hair, ask about your origin, and tease you about your accent? Would you report every incident to HR? Or join them and laugh with them? Secondly, Indian culture puts small things into place.

Sprained ankle? *"Beta kuch nahi hua* (nothing happened). It will get okay on its own."

The reason I feel this attitude works is that India doesn't make a big deal of tiny things. Obviously, this doesn't work when the issue is genuinely serious. But the point is that you can't take yourself too seriously in India. I find that healing. While millions of Americans are taking pills for depression, I sometimes wonder if our '*beta, kuch nahi hua*' culture with lots of physical touch and soothing talks heals small wounds. With the growing amount of awareness concerning mental health in India, and with family support and involvement, seeking help for such issues becomes a lot easier.

That brings us to the topic of loneliness.

Loneliness in India May Be Less

Is loneliness a problem only for single people? In America, there is a sense of relief from loneliness when you're busy getting ready to meet friends. That rush to the mirror to dress up, running to the store for chips, and driving to a friend's party buries the chaotic thoughts that would otherwise bother you. Living with a roommate, a busy life, or a spouse is how loneliness is mitigated in the US.

I was shocked to meet couples who said that they felt lonely. Plenty of married NRI couples expressed that they were bored with the routine, that they wanted the India-ness of neighbors with open doors – neighbors that come to your home to ask for sugar. Single people think marriage might drive away that lonely feeling, and for some time it would. Then it can resurface as something entirely different on a random weekend, many years after you have settled in your four-bedroom home in New Jersey (NJ) with a young baby. A sudden longing for the community feel that India provides. *Could it be possible that every first-immigrant family in America is lonely?*

For the longest time, I thought loneliness is a choice you made. You chose to be lonely in America – you chose to stay home that Saturday night and not date random men; you chose a work field where you have to be at the computer and not meet people. But it's possible that you can also be a victim of loneliness due to your personality, your community, and the society.

If you are the type who enjoys human company, needs constant love, and feeds off the high from others, you are *going* to feel alone in an individualistic society like America. Though there are plenty of NRIs who may say 'Lonely? No. I never felt that way. In fact, I love being alone,' there are plenty of NRIs who also say they feel very lonely. Your personal nature could be built in a way that you need people around you. You could help yourself by changing your environment so that you're in a community-based society rather than living in an individualistic society.

The community culture of India has a nosiness that might annoy you – the aunty on the 3rd floor who asks you to wear saris, the neighbor uncle who comments on your kids, the storeman who knows your mother bought *jamuns* yesterday – the same nosiness that irritates you and me forms the blocks that make the community. It's a different side of the same coin. The beauty of India is that I know that the store uncle will help me if I fall into trouble, that the neighboring uncle will make sure your kids play safely in the compound. I know that the 3rd-floor aunty will offer to feed me on days she's made biryani. This is why loneliness has a milder flavor in India than America. Even though gated communities have less intrusive neighbors who keep their distance, they'll still help. You could possibly be less lonely in India.

The same nosiness that irritates you and me forms the blocks that make Indian community.

This also brings to mind an interesting question. While your Indian neighbors are not worried about spending time, food, and money on you, what is an NRI's relationship with money in India?

India Might Better Your Relationship With Money

We all knew of this friend in Atlanta, who had infamously asked his roommate to return the $2.30 his roommate owed him. Socially he is known as a ***kanjoos*** (miser in English/***kanjan*** in Tamil/***pisinari*** in Telegu/***pishukan*** in Malayalam/***kipte*** in Bengali).

The problem kanjoos people face is that that is all they are remembered for. They may have lent a shoulder to crying friends, held their hair back when they vomited during a night out, or kept a purse to hold a seat at a packed concert, but if the kanjoos hesitated to pay for a coffee once, that is all they will be remembered for. Like the $2.30 guy. Kanjoos people martyr themselves into their friends' 'kanjoos hall of fame' by making small sacrifices to save money. The poor chaps are probably not even aware of their kanjoos-ness.

Plenty of NRIs splurge money, spend unabashedly, buy expensive cars, and will pay for your meal without thinking – we aren't addressing them here. We are discussing the kanjoos NRI.

One may not be an entirely black or white kanjoos; people spend in one area and save in other areas.

There are two types of such NRIs.

The self-sacrificing kanjoos NRI: They spend on friends, but not on themselves – they sacrifice convenience or experiences. My version of this *kanjoosi* was to skip the experience of Starbucks coffee because I lived two blocks from the Google office. *Why should I spend $6 at Starbucks, when I can walk across the street, go up seven floors, and make a latte for myself?* One American colleague would board my office bus every morning with a Starbucks coffee in her hand. I never understood how Americans could spend money on a commodity they were getting for free in office.

What do some NRIs do? Not show up to birthday dinners at restaurants where they'd have to share the bill. I know an NRI who refused to spend $100 for carpet cleaning, even when the home carpets were blackened over six years of living in that apartment. This person was earning $150,000+ a year.

The all-sacrificing kanjoos NRI: This second type of NRI sacrifices their own convenience *and* the money of others for their own benefit. A friend who wishes to stay anonymous narrates, "My wife and I had just bought a house in the NJ area, and we'd started to hang out with a few NRI couples. They turned out to be very miserly. They would choose only cheap restaurants when it was their turn to treat. 'Chipotle this time?' They would order less food: 'Let's do with two instead of three pizzas; it will be too expensive.' They would give cheap tips at restaurants to balance out how much money they had spent on buying a house. While splitting the costs of a potluck, one couple included the price of gas (petrol) for driving to the store and the cost of the time they spent in washing vessels! These couples were all working professionals. We stopped hanging out with them and eventually found friends who were comfortable with spending the same way we did."

Why are some NRIs like this?

Many Indians, like me, have grown up in a middle-class home – ones with mosaic tiles, plastic chairs, and steel vessels with engraved names – with limited money and limited resources. You don't spend money because you simply don't have money. 'Not spending' becomes hardwired. Sacrificing convenience becomes hardwired. When you move to America, you cannot suddenly switch into a 'here, take my money' mode. This makes NRIs hesitant about spending money in their American lives. It's a hesitation hardwired so deep for some NRIs that it doesn't go away even after a decade of earning in dollars.

All these NRIs postpone living a better life. Actually, they don't know *how* to live a better life in America. It's not their fault. The saving money hardwiring is difficult to reprogram.

India might help change that. Here is why:

- NRIs are backed by the power of the dollar to rupee conversion. This allows you to spend on things that feel unaffordable in America. A ₹450 taxi ride might be expensive for locals, but it is cheap to the NRI who returns. The same taxi ride in America will cost $50, which feels very expensive.
- You are probably returning at an older age, to a higher position and higher pay. You possibly have your investments and savings in order. This gives you a buffer of savings to play with.
- Rent is a smaller percentage of your salary in India, allowing you to save more.

- You will observe others spending. In India, even people who don't earn a lot spend on others. You may see co-workers who earn 10% of your salary generously spend on others. A colleague will sponsor paan, someone will pay the rickshaw bill without hesitation, and someone buys coffee for all. ₹15 for a coffee isn't much, but the whole act of generosity becomes a habit. The habit of giving gets inculcated in India, and that reduces the hardwiring.
- You will be spending money everywhere. You will spend on rickshaws, metro, taxis, and Uber. You will spend on rent and for a maid. You will spend on fruits, food, roadside chaat, paan, and pani puri. You will pay for rickshaws or movie tickets and Diet Coke with friends. It's cheap enough that you won't mind, and the spending will become a habit. It's as if your money chakras are opening up, giving you a secret sense of relief from the previous life you've lived with a clogged money pipeline. No longer are you looking at costs or the value of your indulgences and who is ordering what.

Re-wiring takes time, but it does eventually happen. You might not feel richer, but you will be able to lead a better quality of life. So to those NRIs pretending to not have cash at cash-only restaurants or hesitating to book an Uber for friends, here's a reminder: people notice!

Re-wiring spending habits takes time, but it does eventually happen. You might not feel richer, but you will be able to lead a better quality of life.

In India, I am now kanjoos only about Bounty (paper roll). In America, I'd generously waste Bounty and use copious amounts of toilet paper. In India, I'm showing traits of being kanjoos around paper of any kind. No one seems to notice this except my maid, so let's talk about household help next.

Logistical Support Is Better in India

During the years her son was very young, for Piya, from California, the nightmare started at 4:50 PM every day at her office desk. She had no room for error as her son needed to be picked up from 20 miles away. For every five minutes of delay, the day-care charged her $5. She would make it just in time. Her mother's heart would beat loud when she rushed from her desk to drive her car. Her stress would shoot up when she'd roll her car from lane to lane on the unpredictable I-237 traffic. Money. Time. Traffic. It would stress anyone out. The Cinderella chime at 4:50 PM also prevented her from focusing on her career as much as she wanted to.

After an exhausting drive home, she'd be picking up scattered plastic toys, pushing knives through green vegetables, and converting washed clothes into folded laundry mountains. These were tasks that her weekly cleaner could not help with. Her story mirrors how thousands of mothers and fathers in America feel – chained to their Cinderella schedules and to the seats of their SUVs to accommodate soccer practice.

In comparison, logistical support in India is unbeatable. Returned NRIs, with money to spare, surround themselves with the best of services. An in-house cook, in-house 24-7 nanny, driver, and concierge are services availed by those with a higher income. NRIs with smaller disposable incomes can get apps that will, for a price, run errands for you. The app can deliver fresh food, parlor services, or get you a driver for a day – all within your NRI return budget.

Prasanna Ranganathan, who was a senior software engineer at Netflix in California, already had two kids in the US before he moved to India. He is thankful for the extra time freed up by local support in Bangalore. However, he feels this tradeoff between logistical support in India vs. the stressful life in America is all in the mind. He feels that NRIs who have accepted (and believe) that the perks of America are better than of India are willing to go through the hard work – driving to get groceries after a long day at work, doing the laundry, and driving kids to classes. He maintains there is no 'better or worse' but merely a preference.

Dr. Gautam Govitrikar, a dentist who moved to India from NJ, talks about his grocery purchase routine in NJ. He'd button up his kids, strap them in the child car seat, drive ahead while often checking on his kids through the mirrors, get them out of the car, shop, and drive back, all taking at least an hour of his time. In India, he walks to his gate and takes a right turn to see the vegetable vendor with his cart of assorted vegetables. It takes him two minutes to get groceries in India. He is ecstatic about the time this has freed up for him.

I am personally very thankful to have a maid in India. My parents have a maid that comes in two hours a day. She's been with us for more than 12 years and knows me since my college days. Our maid is absolutely stunned at my incompetence in the kitchen, and she enjoys, in a curious sort of way, her mastery over an art that I don't have. She often observes my shenanigans in the kitchen and corrects me: "How are you opening the garlic?" she says. "It not like that. See," and she shows me to deftly open a pod with hands that have been doing this for like a thousand years. On days I'm being lazy, I'll sheepishly ask her to put oil in my hair, and she'll massage it in. This kind of support is a luxury indeed, and I could never dream of it in America.

This logistical support allows you to focus on other things – like taking risky bets, which we will talk about next.

Risky Bets and the Humiliation of Being an Immigrant on a Visa

I started my career in a small American firm. They were sponsoring my H-1B, and I was grateful for that. I was also anxious about its status. One afternoon, I asked the HR manager for an update about my H-1B approval, and he directed his restless anger toward me. He yelled, "I'm not sitting on your H-1B card, dammit! I will let you know when it comes." I felt humiliated. To him, it was a piece of legal paperwork, but to me, and the other NRIs in office, this wasn't just a piece of paper. It was my security toward a future where I could uplift my family from their current economic status to a higher economic stability. It was a piece of paper that would guarantee my freedom to change jobs if I needed to, and that would dictate where I lived and where I went.

Imagine a world without being on an immigrant visa. NRIs could take vacations to actually see the world. They could start their own business. Newlyweds need not fight over their single income and NRIs could fearlessly walk out of bad jobs.

But we have to shake ourselves back to reality. A visa is limiting for NRIs. It not only prevents us from leaving bad jobs, but it also holds us back from expressing ourselves. Bhavna Kapoor, an analytics director who's been in the US for 14 years, told me about how she stood up for herself and her team only now. "I stopped taking crap at work the day I got my green card." A situation we describe here as being *majboor* (helpless).

As an NRI, you will find India to be a low-cost experiment ground. 'I have a startup' is now officially a pickup line in Bangalore.

It has replaced 'I went to IIT' as the coolest thing to do. Many Indians are working in startups. India is also more suitable for risk-taking in personal hobbies. You want to write a book, start a yoga retreat, or join art classes? Do it in India! More now than ever before, India's Gen Z and younger millennials are off on solo trips over India, willing to take a year off from a corporate job. Join them! It's all do-able with minimal repercussions for most NRIs because you can live a year or more in India without an income. The advantage of being in India and having the freedom to try out what you always wanted to makes all the pain of moving worth it.

The advantage of being in India and having the freedom to try out what you always wanted to makes all the pain of moving worth it.

And that brings us to the reasons you might *not* want to move to India and continue where you are.

2

WHY NRIs MAY STAY BACK IN AMERICA

When You Should Stay Back in America

I assumed that all immigrants are fond of their home country. I used to think all NRIs could love India and adjust in India. But this is my truth, and another's truth doesn't have to be the same.

When Seema Sairam followed her husband to India from California, every waking moment she missed America. For her, California was always home. She never wanted to move. She hated her life in India and knew time would not help. She fought hard though – making an effort to adjust to her job, environment, and food. And yet, every experience was a trigger that reminded her of California. Her missing for America was much deeper than mine. My missing was made of jokes and teasing; her missing was made of pain and tears.

How Seema felt is not the result of moving to try things out. This is a result of what will happen if you *know* India is not for you and you still move. You will be miserable.

I would encourage you to keep pushing to continue your stay in America. Wait it out. If America may not feel like home today, it might tomorrow. India might have been home for you at some point, but not today. It's like how you feel when you revisit your college hostel – at some time in your life, that hostel was home, but you might not be able to identify with it anymore.

Open your heart to accepting that America could even be home at different phases in your life. It was for me when I was playing indoor soccer in Atlanta at the age of 23. America was still home for me as a 28-year-old when I played basketball with office colleagues. America might be home for me in the future when I hit 40 and want specialized Pilates classes. America might be home for you in your 20s. It might not be home while in your 30s. And maybe in your 40s, you will feel at home again in America.

Open your heart to accepting that America could even be home at different phases in your life.

Step back to see your life in America and ask yourself: "Is this happiness?" If the answer is a resounding yes, don't even bother to look further into moving to India. If there is an iota of doubt in this happiness ratio – you might then want to explore it. Find your truth.

India has non-trivial problems. We now discuss what NRIs might lose if they move back home. By no means is this exhaustive and by no means can it be true for all, but the list captures struggles you may face with statistically high confidence. This list is like an answer to the question: What could go wrong? It may hold the reasons behind why you might not like India.

Losing Status by Moving to India

"I think you're a ***bewakoof*** to have left America," my aunt blurted out, her index finger jabbed the air in my direction to emphasize the extent of my stupidity. To her, it was clear I was a fool to leave the American dream life. She wasn't the only relative to think so. A month before that accusation, in a dimly lit restaurant, three Edison lights glowing strong above my head, I heard my cousin's aggressive advice. "Go back! *Tumhari kya status hai India mein?* (What status do you have in India?) In America, you'll have status."

For millions living in India, America is the land of fulfilling fantasies. Men think they can have an exotic white girlfriend, women can finally roam in knee-revealing dresses, and adventure seekers can drive a top-down convertible at 120 mph. Indian families want to migrate to America to secure their future. Being in America is like attaining *moksha* for some Indians.

This feeling is amplified with relatives. There is no problem in what they *think*; there is a problem in what they *say*. For you, this might mean that at wedding receptions, 'America' is the name dropping your relatives will do. Your auntie, in her glittering green, over-fitted ghagra, *thali* in one hand and *pallu* propped on the other, will tell unsuspecting strangers, "My nephew lives in California. He is having a big house! His wife works at PayPal. They go on road trips in their BMW."

You, the cousin who went to America, are a hero for the extended family.

The NRI life is seen as the epitome of a successful life for relatives. Anyone visiting India from abroad is given a free welcome kit filled with respect and opinions. Being from America is a weapon the NRI can use to disarm others. Living in America gives credibility. People take you more seriously. For empathy-seeking Indians, it could mean a chance to talk to someone presumably more open-minded. For job-seeking locals, the NRI may have information to help them get a job. For the business-minded, you, the NRI, could mean someone who is exposed to international quality standards (or an opportunity for them to get a 10x price). There is immense power in being an NRI.

If status is your priority, consider staying put in American lands.

This status is important to some NRIs. It might play a crucial part in getting you a good place in the extended family. If you move to India, your status barometer reading may move down a bit. If status is your priority, consider staying put in American lands.

However, if status doesn't bother you, your gender might. What if you're a woman? How will your experience in India be?

Women Lose a Few Freedoms

India has varying degrees of safety for women. Though it is safe to take a taxi from the airport at 11 PM, women generally avoid it. This means that women click on 'sort search results by timing' on booking websites to avoid late-night flights. Not that I've stood behind someone's back watching them clicking around. But I have never seen men restricting themselves to flight timings. If a flight arriving at 1 AM is the cheapest, they'll book it.

I'll controversially remark that it's 20-30% more expensive to be an urban woman in India than being a man. She has to buy expensive flights just to travel in the day time or pay extra money for an intercity taxi, just to use a trusted vendor. This is still a perception problem. Not all places in India have safety issues, but there is a general perception that women must take extra precautions.

The second loss for urban women like me is being limited in the choice of clothes to wear. In my first months back in Bangalore, I wore my dresses and boots but soon felt out of place. I moved to the jeans-tshirt dress code. My colleagues tell me, "Why do you care, Nupur?" but wait, listen to Neha Gupta, a data scientist who's worked in India all her life. She tells me about an uncomfortable incident.

A male co-worker, known for being difficult, verbalized his thoughts on a woman in her 40s, who walked past his desk wearing a pretty dress. He commented to his co-workers, "Why is this aunty trying to look young?" I would have been permanently scarred by such a comment. However, most large companies, MNCs, and startups are cool with any dress code. Just perhaps rethink wearing your boots to the third floor of Sada Bahaar Printing Press in Purana Bazaar.

While your city and office culture will determine what you wear, there is one thing you will lose and it won't matter which city in India you move to – the posh life.

Losing the Posh Life in India

If you fear losing the posh life in America, there is merit to this fear. Will you miss the power of swiping a powerful plastic card at the zippy outlet mall for a sturdy blue office shirt? Will you miss the two-storied tall glass windows of your office through which (as you proudly tell your parents) you can see the grandeur of the decorated reddish rooftops of New York City's east side and the vapor that comes out of them? You can sweep your outstretched hand over this view, with the latest iPhone Air Pods in your ears, and ask yourself: "I have this precious posh view here. Will I miss this if I move to India?"

That you will.

You will miss it. You will not be able to have it. You have to move on. If you don't want to move on, you can still keep up a posh life in India – it's just harder and quite expensive.

Due to non-standard building accessories in India, each building has a different feel to it. Though, if you work in one of those eco-business parks in a metropolis city, you won't be able to tell if you're in the US or India. One place I worked at needed reminders to restock toilet paper, had paan-spit decorated staircases, and rainwater leaking onto the office floor. Definitely not a posh experience.

My posh life was also my power dressing and my expensive outfits – stockings, boots, and Burberry coats. I feared I would miss them, and it turned out to be true. My coats, boots, and Nanette Lepore dresses are tightly packed into an old suitcase, pushed on top of the almirah in my Pune home. I've kept them safely. If I ever move back to America, I might need them.

Ashish Mitra, a Stanford alumnus who is now CEO of his own company in Sydney, has a different take. He says, "There is a difference between Western posh and Indian posh. If you're looking to wear a tuxedo and eat at a Michelin star restaurant, yes, you will miss it in India. However, a dinner at the Taj or Leela is far posher than any dinner I've experienced in the world. Here, a turbaned waiter in a sherwani will serve you butter chicken from a copper *handi,* and you will be treated as a king. Isn't this posh? It's just a different posh."

The Western posh example also extends to food. India has a variety of food, but if you're looking for quick sushi and authentic Mexican food, you'll have to search harder for it in India.

The Western posh life problem extends to the outdoors too.

Missing Out on the Outdoors

"I wish I had the outdoors of the US and the support of India,"

– an NRI

In India, outdoor workouts like walking, trekking, and running are possible in some regions of the city. It's also limited to the right time of the day and whether you can ignore closely speeding vehicles and uprooted sidewalks. Millions of people are okay with it. Would you be okay? I don't know.

On Sunday mornings in Pune, where I am as I write this, I see enthusiasts pushing their heavy legs on newly purchased bicycles. It's not impossible to do outdoors! I am not able to bicycle in India because I'm always waiting for the ideal conditions and also comparing it with California. I run outdoors, but it took me time to get used to the upturned sidewalks and traffic. Actually, that's a lie. I still haven't got used to it. I run because I really, really want to run. When I travel to other cities in India, I seek out friendly runners groups through Facebook and run with them. If you really want to keep up an outdoor activity in India, you will find a way to do it.

The park experience in India is sub-optimal in comparison with American parks. Many Indian cities are dotted with small parks. When I briefly lived in South Delhi in 2017, there was a park outside my rented home. In four minutes, I could take a full round of it. The neighborhood residents – ladies in salwars and shoes and men in trousers – came down to the park to fast or slow walk, and I had to adjust by speedily overtaking them. Are you okay with crowds in the park? Will you compare? By all means do, because there is no comparison! I've rarely seen the US equivalent of sprawling park infrastructure in an urban Indian city.

We will discuss in later chapters how your location in a city matters. In my city, there are options to enjoy the outdoors, but they all are located in another part of town. I wouldn't inch my car over the speed bumps and through morning traffic to get there. I visit that area rarely, only to meet friends. This brings me to the next topic and a very important one. Will you have friends and a social life in India?

Social Circle Loss

If you're older than 30 and hope to find a social circle after moving to India, I should warn you that this is going to be a challenge. Bobby Bedi, 35, was the most popular man I've known in my friend circle. In California, he'd host parties where a hundred guests would turn up. People would hover around him like bees around their sweet honey. He was the master of making friends. Bobby tells me, "I've made all of four friends after moving to India."

Be mentally prepared. For people much older than 30, it is difficult to find a social circle. Age (or maturity) makes you picky anyway, but the pool to choose from decreases as well. This is because most people in their 30s or older have around them a family, extended family, and relatives – they want friends, but they don't need friends. This doesn't mean that you won't find friends; it just means you might find it hard to be a social butterfly if you're in an older age group. This can affect your life, especially if you are single and don't have family around.

However, our young NRIs in their 20s will have no problems as finding friends at the workplace is easy. You'll have more fun at work than you would ever have in America. Office is the place to find a social circle; if you're lucky, you'll find a great group in office. For that, you need an office with your kind of culture. Will you? Let's talk about that.

Work Culture Is Different

If you have worked many years in America, there is an absolute possibility that you may take a long time to adjust to the work culture in India. Hang on, we address work culture in much detail in Chapter 10, but here I want to give you a preview of what you might lose out on.

Though every state in America has a different feel, in all of America, the office culture is pretty standard. Everyone politely (even if unenthusiastically) greets you with 'Heyhowareya?' In India, the variability is high. Some greet, some ignore, and some say hello inconsistently.

American culture ignores hierarchy in some ways. No one calls their managers 'sir,' and everyone addresses each other by the first name. In India, I've been in environments where you address everyone as sir. Guess what, I didn't find it odd, nor did I care. Calling someone by name or addressing them as sir doesn't really matter. What does occur is the variability of reaction – you don't know who'll take offense if you treat them as a peer.

America, specifically society in California, encourages everyone else to adjust to include you. In India, the onus is on *you* to adapt to all types of people. For example, California's Be Inclusive movement trains society to be sensitive and careful of how to talk to others. You can't bump into an old friend and tell them, "Hey, you've become fat." In India, you have to decide and filter what should affect you. So if your friend says, "Hey, you've become fat!" you've got to decide if you want to flare up in anger or roll your eyes and let it go. You'll see this not just at work, but also with your friends and extended family. I am not entirely convinced this culture change is a 'loss,' but I think you ought to be informed.

America, specifically society in California, encourages everyone else to adjust to include you. In India, the onus is on you to adapt to all types of people.

Information, knowledge, and education are essential, and that's another place we have a problem. We have an education access loss in India, which we talk about next.

Education Loss

"I am going to night school in America," I'd jokingly tell my friends while I was taking after-office classes at Stanford on creative writing. On days I had class, my heels would click-clack while I rushed down the office stairs, with workshop printouts hurriedly bunched up in my hand, to catch the bus to Palo Alto. At the calming Stanford campus, I'd walk silently, lost in my daydreams, to the students' center where I'd pick up a Starbucks coffee. Holding on to the warmth of the cup, I'd walk into my classroom. The class was skewed mostly toward women of varying ethnicities. When I'd be done with class, it would be pitch dark outside. I'd sit alone on the platform of the Caltrain station, waiting for the late-night train into the city of San Francisco. This is how I studied writing. Every minute of this whole routine felt like unbound happiness. I was high on education.

Access to good education on varied topics is much better in America than in India. Say, you want to take a class on acting in India. I see two problems. First, it's going to be harder to get around in India because of the infrastructure. You can't do this after-office routine easily. It's not impossible, but it's just not easy. Second, you may find non-trivial differences in quality around how the program is managed – the method of giving feedback, communication about the class, or speed of delivery.

For higher degree education, we can assume education in India will improve magnitudes in a decade or more. But currently, higher education is more welcoming and flexible in America. For children, there are international schools in India that provide global-standard education. However, that marries the child into studying abroad for their undergrad degree. You'll have to choose your priorities. NRIs are fearful of the quality of education their kids might get in India and assume an international school is the only way to bridge that gap.

Prasanna, whom we met before, tells us about how he chose a known devil over an unknown angel by putting his kids through a local school with a domestic curriculum instead of an international school. He says, "I grew up in India on a CBSE curriculum. I believe that my family and parenting will be a bigger influencer and play a more important role in shaping my kids than any school, international or otherwise."

While we've taken a peek at the real losses in India for NRIs, there are some myths about India that I want you to be aware of. Let's look at them in the next chapter.

3

MYTHS AROUND INDIA

Myth 1: I Read The News About India so I Know India

India is not the news. Seated in America, we have an odd idea of what India is about from our accessible sources – the media and family. Media has shown its biases. While I am writing this in the quiet corner of a small cafe in India, my Twitter feed makes it look like India is literally on fire. I am reading a news article about stagnation in India and looking out my window. There is no problem to an urban settler like me. People are buying, selling, and partying, companies are hiring desperately, the airport is bursting with travelers, and life is moving on. The social media perception of India is distorted and skewed to paranoia.

India has to be experienced; observing it from the lens of the media or family might skew your understanding of reality.

An NRI wrote his concerns to me by email: "I shudder to think what my kids will eat in India." The dramatic part of me visualized him looking left and right to ensure privacy, before typing out the next sentence in an electronic whisper. "I got a WhatsApp forward from *Bade Mamaji* that red bricks are powdered to replace red chili pepper in food and colors are injected into brinjal and watermelons!" To this person, I say, "Remember that America is the birthplace of the science of genetically mutated food!"

There is a sizable NRI population that tells others, "I've heard that in India they make you work 15 hours a day. You can't go home before nine, and you have to wear a uniform to work." There are places like these in India, America, and the whole world, and no, you don't have to join them. You have that choice, especially since you will not be on a visa.

All these perceptions make the atmosphere around moving to India look like a step-down. I encourage you to realize that India has to be experienced; watching it from the lens of the media or family might skew your understanding of reality. Don't let the news steal you of a truly unique experience.

Myth 2: People Steal

If San Franciscans leave behind a purse in their car, even in a safe garage, there is a 100% probability of a car break-in – window smashed and wallet stolen. You would walk by that car with a condescending head shake in memory of the stupid driver who left his valuables in eyesight. Just when you think you're immune to theft, your bag of vegetables will get stolen from your doorstep while you left it for just a couple of minutes.

I have seen more burglary in America than in India. In America, many colleagues had their laptops stolen from car trunks. 'I'll be back in five minutes; nothing will happen' was the reason for my manager's $1000 golf club kit to disappear. Bicycle theft is common in America. The busy Market St. in San Francisco famously hosts the phone stealing mafia that snatches mobiles from the hands of people. My phone was stolen from my purse at a crowded restaurant. My apartment building had three homes that were broken into to steal laptops. And yet, there is a sort of paranoid accusation concerning India – 'someone might steal my things.'

In my first few months back in India, I was sure a lot of my belongings would get stolen. I was once asked to leave behind my purse under the seat of a friend's car in Bangalore. Years of instinctively hiding my car belongings in San Francisco had created an in-built defense system. At that moment in Bangalore, I wondered why leaving my purse in the car was a good idea. I had to tear myself away from my precious purse, bidding it a mental, "Goodbye, I love you, it was nice having you." An hour later, when I returned, I stood on my toes and peaked through the rear window. It was still there. I felt the stupidity of accusing Bangalore of being a bigger cheat than San Francisco.

My phone has been safer un-attended at a cafe in India than in a cafe in San Francisco. It angers me when people accuse India. I feel like writing all over the walls of the Internet: Don't you dare call my countrymen stealers.

Myth 3: *Tumse Na Ho Payega*

When we see successful Indians in America, we assume they won't move to India. When they tell us through their rolled-down BMW window, "I want to move to India," we look at their comfortable lives and think, *tumse na ho paayega.* (I'm not sure you can do it.)

We also assume life in India will be difficult for people who don't fit the perfect societal narrative, like unmarried women, divorced men, divorced women, and married couples with arguments. We assume they will have a tough time in India. We advise them that they shouldn't move to India.

The truth is that people with all types of *handicaps*, all sorts of successes, and all stages of happiness move to India. Single mothers, wealthy business people, entrepreneurs with no business plans, senior engineers, couples with older kids, fearless divorced women, fearful divorced women, women with a vision, men with a great a job, happy couples, happy couples with unhappy kids – all combinations of all of them. Maybe we are not a good judge of who can make it in India and who can't. Who will adjust and be successful in India is a truth that can surprise you.

While money is collecting in the bank, age is accumulating as wrinkles on our faces. 'I am too old to move now' says the NRI. The more he stays in America, the deeper his roots grow there. At the same time, he fears that the India he wants to move to is getting more distant. It becomes a battle between the head and the heart and the body.

Don't let anyone tell you that you're too old for anything. The oft-repeated 'it's too late now' needs to be proverbially crumpled and thrown into the fire. When I was 31, I thought it was too late to move to India. Rubbish! I was well past the age when I moved. NRIs of all ages move. Newly graduated folks at 23, American-born Indians at 30, single women at 38, divorced women at 37, couples at 28, couples with kids at 35, 40, 45 – there is no rule around the age for anything in life. If moving is your real answer, then don't worry about your age.

India has to be experienced, and watching it from the media or family might skew your understanding of reality.

I'd love you to brutally squash the mental constraints of age, position, level, and status. Sweep them from the pit of fear in your mind. Promise me that you'll never let outside constraints be a limit for anything you decide to do in your life.

Myth 4: India Is a Third World Country and Is Conservative

Simran Singh and her colleague Jenny had just returned to their New York office after visiting India for a work conference. When Jenny was approaching her work desk, her neighbor swiveled in his chair, raised an eyebrow, and said, "You went to India! Welcome back to civilization!" Simran overheard it. Her heart immediately sank. "Does he really think India is uncivilized?" she asked herself.

"Should I say something? Should I ignore it? Never mind. After all, India is a third world country, isn't it?"

Simran, like many NRIs, might have lived and worked aboard for so long that they aren't aware of the leaps that India has made in many areas. An American who wishes to stay anonymous told me he thought India was like a village – a boring place with nothing to do. The movie *Slumdog Millionaire* solidified his impression of India. His perception changed when he visited. "I was most surprised by the wealth I saw in India."

Almost like my surprise when I went to villages in India. My unspoken reaction to a villager was, *Wait, he's not supposed to know English and how did he know to say 'water table' in English!* All the 200 villages that I visited had mobile phones, smartphones, and 4G network. I met a girl scrolling through Facebook, and she lived in the interiors of the Chambal Valley!

In urban India, apps deliver to your doorstep. The market is competitive, and you can find first-world comfort. Surely, there is a lot of improvement that can be done and is in the works, especially concerning infrastructure and cleanliness, and they are in the process. But I would hesitate to call India a third world country.

Having left India in the early 2000s, some NRIs are stuck in the time when they lived in India. You may be surprised that the younger Indian generation leads a vastly different lifestyle than what you were exposed to. The percentage of youngsters drinking alcohol has gone up; most youngsters I know are regular drinkers. The incidence of female smokers has gone up over the past few decades, and live-in relationships are more common now. I am not saying drinking, smoking, and live-in relationships are what is being open-minded. I am pointing out that it is the opposite of the conservativeness you expect. Incidentally, many NRIs move to India and get a cultural shock – this is not the India they anticipated.

4

LIVING IN DENIAL

Some NRIs will never move back to India, yet continue to think they will move. These NRIs make decisions today on the platform of a future plan without facing the truth – they may never leave America.

Nalini Nair, a UX designer in Texas, can't tell which side she's on. "When I tell people I want to go to India, they think I'm not going to go. I'm not one of those who say it and don't do it!" Then she admits with a laugh, "I've been saying this for eight years now, and I still live in Texas." She may be in denial or she may take a long time to move, we don't know. Only she can introspect.

Shefali Saini, my running buddy, once told me during a particularly long run in California that she had loud and hurtful fights with her husband whenever the topic of India came up. She wanted to move back and he just didn't. I know him. He is the more dominant of the two – they are never moving back. She can't face it. She said, "I've parked the decision and pain behind a closed door, to be opened later." I wish she were to lessen her pain by seeing the reality. The fact is that she may never move back to India. Like Nalini and a million NRIs, she's hanging on to a desperate hope that might never materialize.

I wish she were to lessen her pain by seeing the reality. The fact is that she may never move back to India.

When I announced my departure from America, a co-worker at Google, Anshul Mehendale, was taken aback. He told me admiringly, "I thought you were just all talk. All my friends say they will move, but they never do. And you actually are!" I was afraid to take that as a compliment. Because the decision to leave was built over a million layers and a complex mix of reasons at that phase of my life. Even if one reason was missing, I would have stayed back. Perhaps if I were married, I might have never moved back to India. I would have been the person to say 'I'm moving back' and never move.

So what is the problem with being in denial?

A Confused Indian Says That America Is Residence, But India Is Home

As an NRI in denial, I convinced myself that America is not home. I loved the ease of life in America, but I forced my life to fit a script – the script that India is home.

As a patriotic Indian, I felt a deep-rooted moral responsibility to not accept America as home, kind of like accepting another mother as your mother. Yes, I loved America as a resident. I loved the freedom of designing my life with many options – Like sweeping off gluten-free chips from the Whole Foods shelf into a rolling cart, running in my Nike shorts on a sidewalk at lunchtime, or squeezing in three dinner parties in one night.

But while adopting America as my resident home, I also sprayed my life with Indian confetti and color. I inserted Indian choices into my carefully designed Indian-American life with the hope that it would keep me rooted. I kept my solid Indian spellings of 'colour' as if using American spellings meant showing allegiance to America. I visited chaat cafes and made only Indian friends. I treated American football indifferently as if learning the game meant my roots would grow in America. My denial made me bitter toward America – rejecting American culture and not fully adapting to life there.

Mixed in this emotional NRI cauldron of denial is the fear of the unknown future, the sweet acceptance that you're indeed one of *them* – the ones that didn't go back, the ones that clenched foreign mud and put it to their forehead in reverence reveling in the *mitti ki khushboo* of America – Yes, I know you'll say, "No one is actually going to do that, Nupur. I'm not going outside Walgreens and picking up the wood shavings and putting it to my head. What drama!"

And yet, here you are. With every Diwali potluck dinner, every IKEA bed purchase, standing at Enterprise rent-a-car every July 4th, every monthly GEICO payment, every office promotion, every dollar that gets deposited into that treasure chest of freedom we call the US life, you are growing your roots in that part of the earth. Your home is America, and yet you call India home.

A Confused Indian Might Live Like A Nomad

A common outcome of being in denial is for NRIs to live a nomadic life. If you're one of them nomads, you'd buy cheaper furniture, get a short-term lease, or buy a cheap car because America is not really home.

Ayesha Ansari, from Fremont, can tell you how her husband keeps a naked tube light in the corner of his room instead of investing in a floor lamp. He uses a blue-toned plastic dresser from Walmart in his room, all because he doesn't want to lose money. "If I invest in physical things in America, I might not be able to move to India," Ayesha's husband argues.

Leaving America needs an 'escape velocity.' This escape velocity to leave America is high, and furniture appears to pull you down. Don't you let that worry you. Remember that events like moving countries carry enough escape velocity that no matter how rooted you are – leased BMW, four-bedroom home, Scandinavian furniture – you'll uproot. You will move it or sell it because the move justifies it. When your time is right, the escape velocity will build itself up, and the house, the car, and the furniture will find a new warm owner who will love it as much as you did.

> **If your furniture is taking precedence, your move is not a priority for you at this time in your life. You can safely postpone your decision for a few years.**

If you feel hesitant to move to India because you don't want to sell your dear furniture, the move hasn't gathered enough momentum. Your escape velocity is low. Don't beat yourself up for loving your furniture more than India. Moving to India is not a virtue. It's a decision that comes after many layers of reasons pile up in a phase of your life. If your furniture is taking precedence, your move is not a priority for you at this time in your life. You can safely postpone your decision for a few years.

Because once you decide, furniture will be a logistical issue and not an emotional issue.

A Confused Indian Makes 'Eventually' A Safe Word

Have you heard yourself say, "I am going to move to India, eventually"? I raise my hand here. I said that too. While I had in my mind a distant plan to move back to India, it wasn't clear how or when. But it was a cloudy fact that I would 'eventually' go back. It was a plan so sure that I never gave it an afterthought because the decision always needed to be made tomorrow. And decisions that need to be made tomorrow can be postponed. And they are postponed because the pain isn't worth carrying and the decision is too scary to look in the eye. And that is precisely what I did.

I couldn't accept that I might end up living in America for the rest of my life.

'Eventually' was my shield. Saying that I will eventually move back repelled curious questions from friends or relatives on my intentions to settle down in America. 'Eventually' gave me comfort, like a cold crystal ice cream on a sad night. It calmed down my own fears and masked my denial. There was so much weight in 'eventually' that it became my keyword – I will lose weight, eventually. I will meditate, eventually. I will move back to India, eventually.

I choose to shut the move to India inside the 'eventually' locker because opening that locker churned my stomach. One major obstacle to happiness as an immigrant is living in this denial.

How to Get Out of Confusion and Denial: Getting Real

Kunal Kulkarni, a tallish Mumbai guy from my running group, was a quiet man you would forget easily even after a few meetings. I appreciated him, though, because his realism was stark and burning. He was an actual realist, not the 'there is something better in store for you' kind of advisor.

One weekend, I was seated at a table at a Castro street restaurant in South Bay. A breeze was blowing through my hair gathered in a ponytail when I said, "I'm going home this December," to Kunal, who sat across me. I added, somewhat curiously, "Don't you miss home?" I thought he would for he seemed that sort of guy who would miss his mom's cooking.

It's not what he answered. It was how he answered. He said unhesitatingly, unabashedly, confidently, clearly, and quickly, "Well, now *this* is home," pushing his palm downwards to the concrete California floor.

I wanted to cry. His realism shook me because I was in denial. For the first time, I saw someone fearless about a fact that I myself couldn't face.

For the confused NRI, life in America is bubbling with oscillating emotions. Like a lover tearing petals off a rose – I'll move, I'll not move; I'll move, I'll not move. These emotions are then shoved under the umbrella of 'eventually.'

The reality is that most of you will not move back. I'm sorry to say this and sorry you have to hear this, but a statistically significant number of confused NRIs don't move back. I'd love you to prove you're not part of that statistic. But right now, you can ask yourself: "Am I in denial? Do I dread hearing the five words 'You will settle in America'?"

Face your 'eventually.' If your eventually is to stay in America, face it and digest it. Scream it out loud to yourself in a closed car. America deserves your sincere chance to make it a home. Your heart deserves a chance to not roller coaster through emotions every time your mother calls or you buy curry leaves at the Indian store or you sing the *aarti* on Ganesh Chathurthi pooja. You need to decide now to live your life fully in America.

Face your 'eventually.' If your eventually is to stay in America, face it and digest it. Scream it out loud to yourself in a closed car. America deserves your sincere chance to make it a home.

I Got Real and I Can't Move to India. Now What?

If you have discovered that you should not move, the first thing you need to do is stop worrying. However, if you cannot move due to circumstances and are unhappy and feel stuck, I suggest you make major changes to your life. Live your American life completely and wholeheartedly. Here are some ways you can do that:

1. **Spend the money:** The middle-class script of saving money is hardwired into the desi. Our save mode is always ON. If you are hesitating to book an Uber to save a few dollars or picking up old bread just to save 50 cents, you might be sub-optimal in your living in America. Spend the money and live properly.

2. **Settle down physically:** So go ahead and do the math and then buy that home you always wanted. Invest in a proper bed, invest in good food, and invest in life. If you were to die tomorrow, how should you have lived?

3. **Take your vacations:** Don't bore yourself by saving leaves for the annual December trip to India (where you stay at home and do nothing). Take vacations to travel the world. Take a day off for your birthday. Go to the spa. Take a random Friday off and make it your own long weekend.

4. **Give your job the seriousness it deserves:** If you're working too much, sit back. If you're working less and pouring over WhatsApp all day, take a step back and commit to the job that is paying your rent.

5. **Entertain:** Get your parents or a relative to visit or host an out-of-town friend. It will make you feel at home in America-land.

6. **Get a roommate:** If you're single, no matter what age you are, having a roommate makes a huge difference. There is a smiling face, or at least a face, to come home to.

7. **Step out of the Indian zone:** Try a new cuisine every weekend or go to parties where you'll find people from other parts of the world. Become a global citizen.

8. **Embrace your patriotic sentiments:** You can still be patriotic and contribute to India. Hold the India flag high, for you are a representative of our country. Host an Independence Day party, bust myths about India, wear a bindi or sari to office, or send school fees for your maid's kids in India. Check Chapter Six for more information on patriotism.

The whole experience of America can be different for you, even if one parameter is changed. These small 1% changes can help you move out of denial and into a happier zone. This will put you in a better position to accept that America is your new home.

5

MOVING TO INDIA, A MISTAKE?

Still confused? Perhaps you are not in denial, but you're confused. 'What if I move and don't like it?' This is a question all NRIs ask. Every single one of them. No exceptions.

The decision to move to America is easy. You might approach it analytically, but you don't have to *feel* so much about the decision. This is because the American life is desirable to the whole world. Moving aboard is less of a gut decision – you just do it. You just assume abroad is better. Heck, abroad is even a word for a better life. We've often heard: "This street is so clean, I almost thought I was abroad!" or "Your home looks just like the homes abroad." The word abroad is commonly uttered with reverence. Moving *abroad* is a no-brainer.

However, the reverse flow – moving from abroad to India – is a feeling-based decision. You could analyze your decisions in a spreadsheet, but when you're done with that spreadsheet and are cozy on the couch staring at your TV, you will still want to know if you will like it. *Will I like the work, the food, the travel, the people, the society?*

In this chapter, we will dig deeper into why NRIs fear to make this mistake. We will also discuss the fears of moving back to America – Return To America (RTA). Then we will redefine what success means to help us shrink our fears down to the manageable size of a latte.

You could analyze your decisions in a spreadsheet, but when you're done with that spreadsheet and are cozy on the couch staring at your TV, you will still want to know if you will like it.

Consequences of *Not* Liking It in India

Imagine you've moved to India. Imagine you're admitting to your family, "I can't stand it here!" There may be monetary and logistical consequences of not liking your move to India. We're not addressing that angle. We are addressing two key emotional consequences of not liking India.

Consequence 1: You Don't Like India but Continue to Live in India

Everyone hates their emotions being tossed around by circumstances outside their control. Irritating relatives accusing you, neighbors being rude, shopkeepers cheating you, boss turning out to be a cross-eyed crazy, salary not looking enough in the bank, traffic making you scream – anything could trigger a blaze of anger from your pretentiously calm inner Zen. We all fear a future where we might have emotional pain. This fear is natural and comes up in any circumstance, not even related to being an NRI. Yet you, the returned NRI, will put yourself through an emotional roller coaster, wallowing in a twisting mix of irritation, anger, and pain. We address this point on how to adjust to India in Chapter Nine.

Consequence 2: You Don't Like India, and Decide to Return to America

Imagine you've decided to return to America. You will go through the fears of perceived failure and extra anxiety about finding a job. My tiny sample size is littered with examples of NRIs who moved to India and then moved back to the USA. This second consequence is what we're addressing in this chapter. We will talk about how moving to India doesn't have to be a permanent decision. Yes, a temporary move might also cut the deal for you.

The Permanency of Moving

The Guptas were hosting their own 'The Guptas are returning to India' farewell party at their Sunnyvale home. I kind of liked them even though the wife was a bit of an expensive-purse showoff. I was honestly surprised to hear she was going back. I'd never thought of her as an adjusting sort of person.

I was vacantly staring at her Zara dress, while loosely holding a red plastic party cup in my hand. My friend Hiren, sitting next to me, turned and said, "They all come back."

I put my cup down on the center table, where a badly scribbled farewell card lay open. "So what's wrong with that?" I asked, giving him my full attention.

"They will come back to America," Hiren reasserted. "Just watch. All NRIs come back."

My heart sank a little. I feared he was right. They *do* all come back. Look at the Sharmas and the Subramaniams. They all came back, citing all sorts of reasons – The traffic from Sarjapur road to home was a nightmare; we came back for our son's college education; or Minu didn't like her job.

The painful knot in my stomach was asking me, "If I moved, would that happen to me too? Would I not like it and come back to America?"

When society talks about those who moved back to America after moving to India, the RTAs, people speak of it in the sense of *he tried, but he failed*. The nice ones say, "welcome back." The candid say, "I told you you wouldn't last."

The failure of an RTA is a very public affair because the success of an RTI is also public. You don't go down silently. Moving to India is not an event meant to be dealt with like a long weekend ride to Yosemite National Park. You update your friends about your home sale. You have a countdown clock of 60 days showing on your face. When you hop on the flight, you post a Facebook update of 'After 12 years in the US, I finally....' It's an announcement to the world. This is seen as a homecoming – the return of the successful son/daughter to their homeland. So, it calls for much fanfare on either shore, and the world takes it in as if this was the last ever big decision you will ever make. And this is the problem.

Moving to India is treated as a permanent affair. Like a fairytale story where a long-haired princess meets a prince and they lived happily ever after. This unwritten social pressure makes it harder for NRIs to make a decision.

We need to challenge NRIs on why they view re-returned NRIs as crazy people who lost all their money investing in McDonald's ice cream stocks. As if the decision to return to America makes you a failure of a person! Society thinks about permanency as a measure of success for moving to India.

In reality, we are changing all the time. We have different goals as we change. We will see in Chapter Six, under the section on advice for couples, that NRIs may return to America even when they are happy in India. They may move back to America for any reason – opportunity, position, money, health, finding a spouse, keeping a green card, and so on.

Do What Is Right for You in This Phase of Your Life

When I turn a telescope to my past, I can see that whatever I did was right for that phase of my life. In my student years, I made a stupid choice. I opted to be a martyr by signing up for mechanical engineering instead of computer engineering for a moralistic reason. My father and grandfather were engineers of that kind. It is a decision I regret today. But when I look back at that innocent, curly-haired girl who got no career guidance, couldn't afford new shoes, and reused a small, limited wardrobe for four years of college, I forgive her. That was the best decision she could make at that point, with the limited information and the limited options she had back then. That answer holds true for your move to India. You are making the best decision for yourself in this phase of your life with the limited resources and limited information you have.

Remember, this holds true for your move to India. You are making the best decision for yourself in this phase of your life with the limited resources and limited information you have.

Events like marriage, money, babies, and deaths force us to reprioritize our lives. If any such event occurs, the option of returning to America might present itself to you or me. Then I will, as Indians say, *do the needful.* And so will you. I encourage you to do what is right for this phase of your life.

The only way out of this fear of 'going back may be a mistake' is to understand the temporary nature of phases in life. Today you enjoy one thing, tomorrow another thing. You don't have to stay in India forever. Let's challenge the need for the permanency factor when deciding to move to India. If moving to India is going to be a failure, you might as well fail big.

Am I A Loser to Move to India?

Sometimes I wonder if I am a loser. I mean, what am I doing here in India? I certainly feel like a loser. I don't have a high-profile job. Oh wait, I *left* my high-profile job to move to India. I just broke up with my boyfriend. I am back to being single again, that too at this age. I am a good 10 kg heavier than my US days. I have nothing to show off about. Heck, I even live with my parents. In American culture, that's the definition of a loser – someone who moved back in with their parents.

I sometimes wonder if I left a place or the promise of a life that never happened. I was supposed to have a California house with a pebbled walkway and hooded windows, where I'd pull up the blinds and watch my rich neighbors receive their new teakwood wine cellar shipment. I was supposed to be that girl.

But this is my life now, and I have to accept it.

Am I a loser even in India? I was supposed to earn 60 LPA (lakhs per annum), a salary that everyone anecdotally earns. A salary that society expects I would get. But I don't. As I wipe the dust off my laptop with the side of my palm and look at my screen, I wonder: *if this laptop goes bad, can I still afford these Apple gadgets?* As the single girl who left her dream job and lives with her parents, I wonder: *Am I a total failure?*

And yet, I am happy. Plain, simple happy.

For the first time in my life, I made a choice that catapulted me into a situation that stripped me of all the fluff the world put on me and left me with no choice but to be happy. The frills of being in America, the shine of earning in dollars, the glow of the Google job… it's all gone. And I have nothing left to be superficial about. I am plain, simple happy.

> **For the first time in my life, I made a choice that catapulted me into a situation that stripped me of all the fluff the world put on me and left me with no choice but to be happy.**

If this is failure, it's pretty darn good failure to have. I am here watching my parents grow old. I am showing them the magic of Internet shopping. I am holding wooden ladders for them to climb as they reach into the loft. I am introducing them to the IMAX theaters that they constantly complain about and yet accompany me to. I am watching them as they have given up dyeing their gray hair.

I am not under the illusion that they are immortal – parents have a life span, and I can't pretend they will live forever. When I see my gentle mother's face, the time I've spent with her, and how I'm making her laugh with silly jokes, it makes up for the lack of the god damn success or the money that I could have been making. I have made this opportunity for myself by giving up another life that was supposed to be glamorous. I am loving my failure.

I may be a failure to lose my bling career options, my wealth in dollars, my fitness, and my freedom, and yes, I *do* miss it. Make no mistake, I do miss earning in dollars and my fitness routine. But I've realized I cannot be happy if I continue to judge my life with the metrics that society puts for me. If I don't reset my metric of success, I will be a failure. I have to redefine my success metrics. And this is what you will have to do too.

Change Your Metric for Success

You'll have to redefine your success metrics in India anyway. The disparity in lifestyle in India, mentally, and physically, is stark. No apartment is built the same, no commutes are the same, and no one has the same office circumstances. You cannot compare yourself with others, and you have to understand what success means to you.

But I've realized I cannot be happy if I continue to judge my life with the metrics that society puts for me. If I don't reset my metric of success, I *will* be a failure.

What is success for you? Is it singing out loud in your luxury Lexus? Is it getting organic food at Rainbow Groceries on 14th street? Is it a $200,000 job? Is it merely having a husband? Is it living in a sea-facing, marble-floored apartment in South Mumbai? Or in New York? What is your metric of success?

You might say, "In India, success for me is getting a 50 LPA salary and getting my kids into an IB School."

These are still external dependencies. Can you make this metric more inwards? Think about it.

Maybe success is not about the 50 LPA but feeling content despite any salary. Success is being stress-free. Success is being healthy, mentally and physically.

Don't fall for the trap that these don't sound exciting, that they are not Instagram worthy. There are no numbers or scores to keep. These internal success metrics are the only metrics that will guide you correctly. Internal success means internal progress, which is not visible to the eye.

Unfortunately, society wants to see visible progress. They don't care if you have changed as a person. They want to see tangible numbers. They want to hear 60 LPA salary. They want to hear Engineering Director or Founder, CEO. Society wants to see success but as defined by externally-driven and visible metrics. If making progress is success, then going to America is success. By that definition, moving to India should also be a success. But not in the eyes of society – not for the auntie whose son lives in Idaho or the friends who pride themselves for their aerial gymnastics class in Boston. For the majority, America is still a success and moving to India is still because of a problem.

If you want to neutrally judge your move to India, don't work by society's metric; work by yours. Find out the type of life you want to lead and find out if you will be successful in designing that life in India. Focusing on designing a good life will make sure your move to India is smooth and free from unwanted emotions – free from hurt, pain, irritation, and anger. Judge your life by the quality of your feelings and not by the measure of money, status, or power.

> If you want to neutrally judge your move to India, **don't work by society's metric; work by yours.**

How to Position Your Move to Society

Ironically, while we're discussing how to ignore society, let's now discuss how to *not* ignore them and how to position your move to society.

When you moved to America, you didn't explain your decision to your neighbors. You just trusted life and moved ahead. Honestly, do the same for moving to India. You don't have to justify your move to anyone.

However, with today's social media, telling the world you're moving to India might also be a societal necessity. Else you'll get angry voice calls of *'Tumne mujhe bataane ki zarroorat ni samjhi?*

(You didn't bother telling us!)'

An easy way out of this societal pressure is to use a script that factors in non-permanency. Some examples of what works and doesn't.

'We are returning to India' – No!

This statement looks like you're walking into a sad black hole from which you can never come out. Vinayak Nagpal, CEO of a startup in Berkeley, is adamant, "You are merely *moving* to India. You are not *returning* anywhere. India isn't even the same India that you left. So you're not *going back*. If at all, you're going forward!"

'We want to try India' – Hmm...

This script is just okay. It covers the non-permanency of your move. It's a comforting script for you but not for society. Try is a word that assumes there is a success and a failure. Success if you stay and failure if you return to America. It sounds like you're trying to fail. Scratch that!

'We are moving to India' – Yes

'We are moving to India to enjoy it for a few years' – Yes!

This is much better and more positive for you. You don't have the pressure to stay if things don't work out. And society sees that you are clearly aware of the exploring you want to do in India.

If I Move, What Is the Guarantee I Will Stay?

SCENE, Breaking Bad, Season 03, Episode 07

VIEW OF A PLAYGROUND

(We see twin boys - Mexican, about 10 years old - chasing each other on the playground as their uncle watches from a chair. The twins start to fight. Brother Two beheads the toy of Brother One. Brother One runs to the uncle in anger)

BROTHER ONE: (ANGRY)

"He broke my toy!"

UNCLE:

"He was just having fun. (Pause) You'll get over it."

BROTHER ONE:

"No! I hate him! I wish he was dead!"

(Camera shows uncle thinking for a few seconds with cold eyes)

UNCLE:

whistles

(Uncle indicates to Brother Two to come over. Brother Two walks close to the uncle)

UNCLE:

"Get me a beer bottle."

(As Brother Two bends over the tub of ice water, the Uncle dunks his head into it, forcing him down. Boy struggles maniacally)

UNCLE (looks at Brother One):

"This is what you wanted. Your brother dead. Right?"

(Brother One hits his uncle's hand. He fights hard to get him to release Brother Two. The uncle doesn't budge)

UNCLE (in a cold voice):

"Try harder if you want him alive."

(Brother One punches his uncle in the face. The uncle frees the boy. Brother Two is gasping to gather his breath, and both twins look at their uncle. The uncle turns to them and says only one thing.)

UNCLE:

"Family is all."

'If I move to India, what is the guarantee I will stay?' asks the NRI. When all your fingers are pointing to a future in India, you might be fearful that you won't last. We have previously addressed that the need for permanency is not required. You really don't have to last, but right now, we're going to talk about a reason that will make you have a better bonding with India. That reason is your anchor.

Just like a heavy anchor holds down a restless iron ship, we humans need an anchor to settle and be unshakable at our ports.

America has a suite of offerings for anchors that have helped immigrants settle there. It's usually a combination of job, purchasing power, exponential wealth generation, ease of life, health, and fitness opportunities. For India, the strength of the anchor depends on the weight of emotion attached to it – how emotionally invested are you in the anchor?

For most NRIs, their anchor in India is family. And family (as we saw in the *Breaking Bad* scene) is everything. If the anchor is strong, like family bonds, settling back and building a life in India is easier. Being with family gives you a constant, unchanging higher goal.

One could argue that if you had family in Singapore, then would you feel the same way about moving to India? Probably not.

Home is where your family is. But India has some anchors that are exclusive to India, which are culture and language. NRIs want that exposure for their kids. Some NRIs find an anchor in India's community-based support system or in a spiritual life – an offering deep in the fabric of India. Family plus culture makes for a very strong anchor combination. The stronger your anchor, the stronger is your answer to 'Why India?' The stronger your reason for 'Why India?' the stronger your will to commit.

Mild anchors are those that are strong initially but weaken over time. Mild anchors are still legitimate anchors because, often, we need to get it out of our system – *bhoot utar gaya* (we address this briefly again in Chapter Six under the topic of Couples). Goals like writing a book, spiritual and travel exploration, starting an NGO, or a step up in the career track could be mild anchors. Once you're done with them, you'll restlessly drum your fingers on the table and ask, "What's next?"

The stronger your anchor, the stronger is your answer to 'Why India?' The stronger your reason for 'Why India?' the stronger your will to commit.

I personally got book writing and social work out of my system. Once I was done with all these activities, I calmed the fuck down. I swear. I felt relieved that I had tried what I'd been wanting to for a long a long time. If luck isn't on your side, mild anchors might not work out for you. You'll have a poor experience, and you'll wonder why you moved in the first place.

A combination of anchors would be the best for a smooth moving and settling experience. For many it is family and love for the country. Ask yourself how strong your anchor is.

6

TYPES OF NRIs AND ADVICE FOR THEM

In this chapter, we discuss different types of NRIs and advise them on making the decision to move or not. Which type of NRI category do you fit into? The list is not exhaustive, but there is one key part to remember. I can't emphasize this enough – your likes and dislikes will change with time.

There is a different answer for a different phase of life. You might love your bold life today and be bored with your bland life in five years. You'll fit into one category today, in another tomorrow, and in a third in a few years. So, take these points as indicative guidelines. Use them to examine your situation and priorities. But ultimately, decide based on what *you* think is right for *you*.

Types of NRIs by Likes and Dislikes

You Do Not Like India

You are an NRI who comfortably cooks tofurkey on Thanksgiving and is exceptionally happy with your four-bedroom home. You've typed 'Not sure I can take the crowds in India anymore' in a Facebook comment at some point. You haven't visited India in four years. When you do visit India, you feel okayish or feel out of place. Home is not your India home anymore. For you, bliss is closing your eyes under the hot shower of a spacious bathroom with freshly fluffed towels in your American home. You guessed right – you will never move back. You, in fact, should not move. You are in a good place, so stay put. You may find little or no happiness in a move.

You Like India, But Don't Really Want to Move

There are quite a few of you around. You know more about the visa process than your company lawyer. You work toward a US citizenship. You have nostalgic moments about your childhood –

times when you used to play cards with cousins while the electricity was out. But when you visit India, there is a brief moment when the lights go out, and you wonder, *How can I ever live here again?* For the most part, you breathe America – you follow American politics, news, and sports. You have a job that you probably don't madly love. But it's been so long being in an okay-okay job, that you're used to it now. An okayish job in America is better than the possibilities of what you could get in India. NRIs like you could possibly adjust in India, but I wouldn't recommend you move unless something compels you to. Try to stay put as much as possible. I mean well when I say that staying in America is likely to be the happier choice for you.

You Are Confused About Moving to India

This whole book is written for you, actually. If you are a confused NRI, you are probably suffering intermittently. You look forward to visiting India, are nervous when you reach the airport in America, and wonder if it was a good idea to book this trip. But when you're in India, you feel relaxed. You have spoken to many people about moving, and you hesitate buying a house because deep down you want to move to India.

NRIs in this bucket need to carefully evaluate if the move will be fruitful. This is a tough one, so Chapter Seven will address how to make a good decision, even if it means *not* moving.

You Are Not Confused and Want to Move 'Eventually'

As an 'eventually' NRI, you are confident you'll move. Still, there is a high possibility that you aren't facing reality and are in denial of the fact that you might never move. You might be pushing your confusion behind the curtains of eventually. Telling people 'I am going to move' means nothing. They will just stop taking you seriously, like they do a friend who promises to return a book borrowed two years ago.

Deciding if you are in this category requires being honest with yourself. I would suggest that you first stop telling people you want to move, including your spouse. Lock yourself into a *vipassana* (10-day meditation retreat) or go alone for a nice vacation, away from your phone and external influences. Then ask your heart if moving is the answer. Is *eventually* your comfort zone? For those who really know they will move, it's just a matter of time. *When* is the key. We address how one gets to this 'tipping point' to move in Chapter Eight.

You Have Decided to Move

You are an NRI that has decided to move. Your actions are on – you are looking for jobs and talking to people actively about their experiences. This category has the calmest spot, which is when you have booked your flight. There is a sort of relief in making that decision.

Be careful here. Many NRIs actively search for a job and abandon the move after seeing their salary offer. This is an exploration you shouldn't be shy about. You're merely searching for answers, and with more information, you can choose which road to take in this period of your life. Simply recalibrate which bucket type (mentioned in this chapter) you're in.

Types of NRIs by Relationship Status

Singles

This is a thoroughly terrible status to be in in America. I am saying this because I was in this rocky boat that never seemed to find the shore. The problem is not that you're stuck. The problem is that you have the freedom to do whatever the hell you want. There are so many paths to take, and any decision makes you wonder if the other path was better. There is only one conclusion to make here. If you do decide to move to India, do *not* limit yourself because of your marital status or your age. People of all ages, relationship statuses, whether single or divorced, move to India.

In a Dating Relationship

America is a great place for dating. Long weekend drives, trying new dimly lit restaurants, gambling in Vegas – what fun! If you are dating someone, it is best to stay in America and experience all that America has to offer. Moving locations probably doesn't make sense unless it's something you both want to do together.

Couples

NRI couples are perhaps the most miserable when one spouse wants to move and the other doesn't. I invite you to peek into Mohit and Manali Mittal's lives. The two got married in a December wedding in India. Mohit then flew Manali to Chicago on an H4 dependent visa.

Mohit had the best combination at work – he loved his job and he was good at it. It gave him a kick of sorts when his VP would walk past his desk in his shining shoes and wave his hand with a casual, "Mohit, do you have a minute?" Mohit loved being important at work. He was on a trajectory for a great rating and a promotion.

Meanwhile, Manali hated her life. Her visa allowed her only as much as to drive a car around and shop groceries. Manali wanted to move back to India. She missed her parents, her job, and the noise. She blamed Mohit for the life she was living. "If I knew I had to just cook for you, I would have never come here." Her parents had another solution for her: "Beta, once you have kids, everything will be okay." That irritated her, but it was true; after all, she had a friend who stopped complaining once the first child came through. But Manali wasn't ready for kids yet. She wanted to realize her own desires – professional and personal – that she had left behind in India when she moved.

It was a year into their marriage, and Mohit found her frequent tearing up ridiculous. He'd come home from work, and she would be there, crying by the window with her legs folded up against her body. "Why this drama? We are not going to move to India, period."

Thousands of married NRIs in America might find familiarity in this story. There were many different ways Mohit could work this out. He could tell Manali to get a master's degree or take up volunteering in a local NGO.

Now, I want to add one more to this. He could tell her, "You go back to India for a bit."

Hear me out. When NRIs move to India, the possibility of wanting to return to America is high. From my survey, 60% of NRIs who have moved to India, want to try returning to America, *even* if they are happy in India. Let that sink in. This is a *huge* finding.

I've been told in confidence by NRIs who have returned that they visited America some years later to see if I would be able to settle down there again. This includes me. When I was visiting a few years ago, I thought about it. After a few rounds of Santa Clara in the front seat of my friend's car, my heart clearly said the answer was a no – not at this time. Maybe in the future, but not now.

Couples who are arguing over a move can let their spouse move. I know it's high risk. But there is a chance. When the spouse who has moved is content with how much they have explored, whether two months, one year, two years, or longer, they will want to reconsider: "Let me try America again." This option may be worth a try if you have tried everything else possible.

From my survey, 60% of NRIs who have moved to India, want to try returning to America, *even* if they are happy in India. Let that sink in. This is a *huge* finding.

Long-distance relationships are hard anyway, and America-India ones top the list. This is because of the time zone difference of 13 hours, the short overlap of waking hours, and the long travel time to get to the other side of the planet physically. Many NRIs find a way to work it. The spouse travels to India and works from home for a month, frequently travels every year, or does long video conferences every morning and night. At the core of this is the certainty that when you want to make it work, you will.

In Manali's case, she moved to India for an indefinite time. She worked on multiple ideas, got a business started, traveled, trekked, and pursued her dreams. After three years – a time that varies or never comes for some people – she felt satiated and satisfied with what she had achieved. She felt ready and comfortable to move back to America to try her life there again with Mohit.

There is a saying in Hindi, *bhoot utar gaya,* which means that the mad passion you had for something has worn off (we saw this in Chapter Five). Your goal for being in India could be achieved, and you could very well feel that you've exhausted your dreams. If moving to India is one of the '100 things to do before I die', you might feel well in line to return to America, refreshed, and satisfied. Unfortunately, you cannot predict if your *bhoot* will come off. It has to be done to know.

Couples who are not in agreement have to make difficult choices. They need to either park their fights and learn to live in reality – the reality that they might never move – or give the spouse a chance to move on their own and try things out. Do what is right for you, at the right time, and don't care about what society might say about your marriage. Public memory is short-lived.

Families With Children

Dr. Deepali Bhate, an NRI from Albany, NY, who is currently heading research at Boeing, moved to Mumbai with her six-year-old son. His first day at school in Mumbai made his little eyes tear up. "Mumma, the boys in school push me." She wiped his tears with her palm and asked him to brave it out for a few days. It took her a few weeks to understand what exactly he meant. The small Mumbai space and the crowded classroom made the children walk close to each other, which her son misunderstood as being pushed around. She was afraid about her son adjusting, but it wasn't even a month when her son began to enjoy the new school as he made new friends.

"It's not the kids, it's us. It's adults that need time to adjust."

Deepali laughs when I ask her about children adjusting. "It's not the kids, it's us. It's adults that need time to adjust." Sameer Dixit, who now heads Analytics and AI-ML at Persistent Systems, moved from Washington DC and agrees with this. He adds, "Children adjust very easily, partially because it's the adults that have responsibilities. Children simply have to make new friends, and they're good to go."

Sameer has no regrets moving to India, but he points out some disadvantages. "My daughter is a US citizen. We may have to pay 10 times the fees when she enrolls in a university in India." Sameer isn't worrying about it just yet. He speaks of another disadvantage, which is a shocking revelation. "I've noticed that Indian kids feel a little overwhelmed when they converse with NRI kids."

This might be a two-way street here. Indian teens may feel under-confident, and some NRI teens may feel one-up because they are more eloquent and articulate.

For NRIs moving back with kids, it would be best to have grandparents around. Not the visiting type of grandparents but the living-in grandparents. A top researcher at an MNC, who wishes to stay anonymous, tells me, "Not only is my daughter learning rituals like doing pooja from her grandmother, even I am learning!" Deepali Bhate adds one more advantage for her son. "My son's learning different languages with his grandparents around."

Kiran Bapna, head of Startup Partnerships at Google, Bangalore, has her busy home echoing with the voices of her teenagers and their 90-year-old grandmother. She loves that her children are seeing a nurturing of other relationships, an opportunity they would have missed had she stayed back in the US. She tells me, "As teenagers, it's natural they will be only focused on themselves. With their grandmother in the home, they witness relationships beyond them."

If you have children, the best advice we can conclude from all these experiences is that you should focus on how *you* will adjust in India. Your kids will adjust faster than you. For more information on salary and education, read on to Chapters Eight and Nine, where we talk about adjusting to India.

Financial Dependencies

If you have financial dependencies or parents who're plugging a leaky roof in your hometown with the money you send, you might want to focus on earning those dollars and not move to India.

Don't mistake frugality for financial dependencies. If you are pretending you can't find your purse while paying for parking (true story) or you excuse yourself for the restroom when the waiter brings the check (true story), you are just being kanjoos. You are not financially dependent.

Also, having children, a spouse, and a house do not make you financially tied up the way you think. You can sell your home. You will get a new job in India to feed your family. Moving with the family is about disruption more than finances.

If you are clear about this and don't have major financial commitments, then there is no thinking here. You can move to any part of the world!

Types of NRIs by Visa Status

Students

There are three types of students – a poor graduate student, the Ph.D., and the older MBA student. Their theme is not common here. Many Ph.D. students move to India directly after completing their studies for opportunities in research and academia in India. A Ph.D. student may not have a loan on their shoulders, unlike the poor graduate student and MBA student. This financial constraint crushes moving plans for the simple reason – the money earned in dollars pays off a loan faster than Indian rupees. For you, I'd say America is a better place to get some international work experience and pay off that loan.

Recent Graduates

If you're at your first job or younger than 26 and you really miss India, I suggest hanging in there. A job change, a city change, making more friends, and even having a boy/girlfriend, can make a difference in how you feel about living in the US. Amit Bhargava, head of sales operations in an IT firm in Pune, has worked mostly in India and lived abroad for a brief period. He advises youngsters: "If you can, continue to stay abroad at least for 2-3 years just to break even financially. Or at least five years to gain international work experience. Especially if you're in banking, finance, or consulting, the global knowledge will be handy."

Still, if you do have to move to India, there is a bright side. Working in India while you're in your 20s is great. There is a massive pool of friends to choose from, and you might quite enjoy it. However, unless you're breaking down, I'd recommend staying back to build up a decent buffer in your bank. You'll be thankful for this buffer if you do move in your later years. Again, these are indicative guidelines, and nothing is set in stone. Choose what your gut tells you to do.

H-1B and Other Visas

Moving to India while on an H-1B visa is crippling because it's a one-way street – you can't move back to America. NRIs who absolutely want to stay in America have conjured up spectacularly long-winded plans on seeing their looming visa issues. "I will move to India with my current company. Then I will find a job in an MNC. Then I will do an internal transfer to go abroad again." One man predicted: "I will find a job in like Google or Facebook in India and then move to their HQ in America." These are long shots. Unless you are in demand with a Stanford Ph.D. or MIT degree, don't put your bets on such unborn future plans, where your happiness is in the hands of someone taking your interview on their bad day.

> **Artificial constraints like visas should not stop you from living the life you deserve.**

If you are on an H-1B and miserable, should you let America dictate your happiness? Artificial constraints like visas should not stop you from living the life you deserve. Also, as we saw, America is not the only place to migrate to. If residing outside India is your goal, you can move to visa-friendly countries like Canada, Australia, Dubai, Singapore, Hong Kong, or London. If we really want to end up in America, we could say that we will find a way to return to America, but this is simply solace. It's not easy to move back to the US after an H-1B, and it's a truth one has to face.

NRI on a Green Card

Getting a green card is on an asymptotic curve these days. You have no assurance of how long you will be waiting for it. However, a green card makes the decision to move exponentially easier – as you can move back to America, unlike the constraints around an H-1B. There is one downside to this though. To stay outside America, you have to get on a 're-entry permit,' which allows you (facts at the time of writing this book) to stay in India for a few years, plus a few renewals. For each renewal, you have to be physically present in the US for a substantial amount of time (3-5 weeks). In the bigger picture, it's not a big deal. If you're looking to move to India on a green card, by all means, give it a shot. This permit gives you many years to enjoy India – until you decide if you want to RTA or remain in India.

US Citizen

Being a US citizen is by far more relaxed in terms of decision making and easier on the nerves. You can RTA anytime! I would suggest – move unabashedly! The only downside to being a citizen in India is that you have to still file taxes in America and that you can't vote for Indian elections. If you have children and they are US citizens, there may be a bottleneck past their 12th standard in terms of university selection and fees. Make sure you understand this before you dive into India.

American-Born *Confused* Desis (ABCDs)

There's a wide range of American-born Indians. My writing buddy, Aditi, grew up in America, and I suspect a person like her could adjust in India easily. She is more Indian than me! She speaks a sweet Hindi (addresses herself as ***humein***) and has even lived in an ashram in India.

But meet Shana Singh, who grew up in America. She was visiting family in India after she graduated from university and decided to move permanently to India. Shana confesses, "Having grown up in America, I was quite snobby about India. After living here, my perspective has changed drastically. Having immersed myself in the culture and the people, I am more grounded than before. And people are very, very warm here." Shana feels, "Experiencing India as an adult will create a shift of perspective and a positive change for any Indian-born American who feels caught in between two worlds and cultures."

Shana is in a unique position to advise us, as after three years in India, she's seen so much. Her biggest challenge is her accent. "It gives me away. Sometimes I shy away from speaking in a cab, as I have this unfounded fear that the driver will think I'm an easy target to cheat." She smiles and adds, "Also, some people make fun of my accent. The other day someone laughed at how I said 'charger.' Being put on the other side of a pronunciation joke is actually quite humbling."

It's a difficult adjustment to live in India, but with some help and close relatives, it's not impossible for an American-born Indian to move to India.

The Patriotic NRI

"I want to go back to India and do something for my country."

– Many, many NRIs

From my survey of NRIs, patriotism ranked high as a reason to move to India. 'I want to do something for my country' was a constant.

The NRI is upbeat about social causes. He wants to be that guy that harvests water in a remote village. He wants to be Sunny Deol of India, defending poor people in court shouting '*tareeq pe tareeq*.' He cries during the national anthem. He is almost guilty: 'How can I eat so much food when someone in India is hungry?' He becomes a Facebook warrior on Indian politics. He has an opinion on how the CM could have easily won the Satna district in the MP state elections, and he thinks that he will contest one day.

All these are noble thoughts, but are they realistic?

I was the NRI who wanted to help my country so badly that I felt India *needed* me, and I could help Indians do things *better*. I left my job and worked in villages, in the government, and in NGOs. I had great experiences discovering India, but mostly, discovering myself.

The big question is, do you have to move to India to help India?

Doing something for the country from America obviously feels less fulfilling than directly working in the country. The big question is do you have to move to India to help India? I will clear some misunderstandings about helping the country and give you some actionable ideas.

There are three points you need to consider if you want to leap into India to help the country.

1. Is there a chance you need help or introspection yourself?
2. Is it a fantasy to help the country, or are you already working on something?
3. If you could volunteer from abroad and feel fulfilled, would you still want to move?

Who Says They Need Your Help in India? Maybe You Need Help

It could be possible that India doesn't need you. You need India's help.

When I visited villages in India, I was excited to lend my help, because being villagers, wouldn't they be sad and unhappy? I watched their lives closely – the happy colors of their homes painted bright blue, the green paddy fields where their rice grew, the moos from the cows who were the sustenance of the villagers' daily life, and the tea stalls where villagers gathered to talk to their friendly neighbors.

These villagers had sincere problems that would paralyze us urban dwellers. "To get water, we have to walk two kilometers, till there," said one villager to me, pointing his hand toward a distant pump powered by a solar panel. They are so accepting of life and death. If someone died, their grieving was open, and the whole family and whole village grieved together. There was no place for permanent sadness.

I realized villagers in India were happier than I was. I needed to learn from them on how to be accepting of life and to figure myself out before I go on a goal, over-infused with the nobility of 'teaching Indians the right way.' They already knew the right way – I didn't.

Helping the underprivileged can make your life feel more positive, meaningful, and purposeful. For those who fantasize about it, ask yourself, "Are you helping India because you need to be active in social service to feel more fulfilled?"

Is It a Fantasy? Judge Yourself by Actions and Not Thoughts

Are you doing social volunteering in your head?

Do you say yes to volunteering events, and then ditch because you need to finish laundry? Do you, perhaps, aim to volunteer when you visit India, but it's all forgotten when you get to your parents' home? Do you then do mild charity? You tell drivers to keep the change and give a tip to your parents' maid when you leave for the international airport. If you are in this category, moving to India with the goal of helping the country might be a weak strategy right now.

Volunteering is a tough commitment; donating online is easier than going out in the cold to volunteer. This means something for NRIs who're looking to volunteer in India. It might be difficult for you to physically help, even after you move to India. Be realistic in your self-expectations.

You could argue: "What if I become an exception? Maybe this move to India helps me figure things out, and I become Sunny Deol fighting for court dates?" The deal is not about 'can do or cannot do.' The deal is about expectations and subsequent disappointment. Moving to India for social causes, when you aren't already doing something moderate or significant, might leave you disappointed with your helping India goals. This rule is applicable in most jobs too. You have to be already doing that job, to get the job you want.

So first prove it to *yourself* in America. We will discuss how you can do that now, and no, it's not by being a parking volunteer for a San Jose Convention Center concert.

How to Actually Help India?

After Moving to India

1. **Work with an NGO**

   I know some NRIs who spent a year teaching in villages or undertaking social projects in the Himalayas. NRIs who are ready to live a life of giving back in India can be comforted with the thought that anything that comes out of such a venture *has* to be successful. If the venture flies and you enjoy it, the goal is achieved. If it fails, you've gathered beautiful experiences along the way and become a better person. Building a better you is still helping the universe.

2. **Know the local problems**

   The Mumbai Versova beach clean-up is a famous project. It made the leader, a young Mumbai man, famous too. Why was he able to do it and not you, the resourceful NRI? Because he was local. He knew the problem, the people, and the area, and he was dedicated to it for the long term. So what can you learn from this? The best place to start is where you grew up as a local or start an initiative with a local. Sadhguru has famously said: "Intelligent people do what they love. A genius does what is needed."

3. **Just existing is impactful in India**

   Don't underestimate the power of just merely existing. It sounds funny, but with your presence in India, you will hire services – from the maid, driver, parlor, vegetable vendor – and that helps the economy. You might not be assisting in the way *you* want to, but you can help in the way *they* need you to by giving them jobs.

Always remember that when you're confused, don't move!

You might not be assisting in the way *you* want to, but you can help in the way *they* need you to by giving them jobs.

Help While Visiting India

Don't do the instant gratification of helping the 'poor things.' NRIs and foreigners express a heart-melting pain on seeing torn-clothed beggars and hand over money to them. This act, though satisfying, is an instant gratification one needs to rethink. A tea seller once saw that I worriedly gave money to a pitiable woman carrying a crumpled doctor's prescription. He called out, "Madam, she has been using that prescription paper to beg for two years. As a rule, if they have hands and legs, don't give them money, because they should work." Try not to dole out cash for free, as much as you are clouded with pity, guilt, or anger.

Your annual India visit has opportunities to do helpful work. Some examples are:

- Set up a water booth for passers-by in the burning hot summer.
- Clean up a street in your city. Search Facebook for clean-up events.
- Donate blood. Search on Twitter for #blooddonation and your city name.
- Help set up mobile wallet payment for a street vendor.
- Vote! It's a privilege and the most impactful way to help – overlap your vacation with voting day.
- Stop bargaining! Foreigners and NRIs bargain with the trinket vendor and food stall man, and then give money generously to beggars. The reason given for this oddity is 'we don't like being cheated.' I don't too. But how about casting aside 10% of your shopping toward a 'cheating buffer' for these people who earn only from tourism?

- Pay school fees. If your family in India has a maid who has kids, pay their school fees! Don't give it in their hand; go to their school and pay it. A word of caution, they might expect the fees to be paid every year.

Helping From America

Show up at events where your presence makes a difference.

There is an absence of patriotic NRIs at lectures organized by local US busybodies, by 'experts' who talk badly about India. These experts abuse India, use selective arguments to prove a point, and make Indians look like a bunch of mad people. I know, because I've been to these events. I was shaking with anger at the end of them. We need NRIs to show up because standing up for your country and representing your people is important.

But I'm afraid many won't do this. It's not easy to prioritize an angering lecture over wine and cheese with friends at Dolores Park on a Saturday evening. I get it. But this is what impact is about. If you want to make a difference while living abroad, track these hate lectures and show up.

Other Activities You Could Do While Still Living Abroad

- Write to the Indian consulate in your city and ask them to conduct events or host international yoga day.
- Organize events in the temple. I had organized a vegan cooking session in the ISKCON temple in California, and it was well-received.
- If you're a startup kind of individual, set up an India office and hire locals. More impactful would be to hire talent from tier-three cities.

- Promote authenticity. In the office, you can wear your culture on you. Wear a bindi or sindoor to office.

I tried my personal expression of patriotism, and I feel fulfilled now. But, I do look back and see how I did so many things – some impactful, some not. Moving to India for patriotic reasons is noble, and can work out if you have the correct expectations. If you must stay in America, remove the feeling of guilt and still be patriotic by expressing it in your own way.

7

GETTING CLOSER TO A DECISION

"Mumbai's traffic has become worse since I left for America. I don't know if I can live in Mumbai again!"

– An NRI who moved abroad 18 months ago

How to Decide If India Is for Me

I have some bad news for you. There is no single way to decide if you should move to India. There is no template, checkbox sheet, rule book, or god person to follow and find yourself transported into a decision. You have to slowly get to a point where you decide to commit to it and go with it. Moving to India is like an arranged marriage – you collect enough information, decide this is for you, and then commit to it. You may be disappointed to hear this and wish someone could give you a binary feeling about it. The truth is there is no binary TRUE/FALSE variable or RIGHT/WRONG in this.

Moving to India is committing to an experience. Do you go wild and jump in or stay conservative and take your time to make a move? You decide. What the following chapters will help you with is to get you more information to move closer to a decision to move or eliminate moving.

Moving to India is like an arranged marriage – you collect enough information, decide this is for you, and then commit to it.

Compilation: Steps to Decide

If I had a rough day in the US, I would call Mom and pour out my worries, while pacing up and down on the wooden floor of my small

San Francisco apartment. My grandmother would occasionally take the white land-line phone into her wrinkled hands and tell me, "*Beta, paachi aavi ja*! (Come back!)" I was silent every time. I wanted to move but didn't feel like moving just yet. How could I decide? How could I know it was the right thing to do?

When NRIs sign up for a session with me, over the grainy video conference, I take their curious minds through a few points specific to their situation to help them make a decision. Allow me to walk you through some points, which can be generalized to a larger audience. I am afraid you may find this chapter boring, like that material science chapter on elasticity or a medical book with no images. But it has to be done. So as a treat, in the chapters after this, I will tell you about parameters you should *not* use to decide.

1. **Loving America:** In which direction is the wind of love pointing your weather vane to? List out what you love and hate about America. List out what you love and hate about India. Which spectrum are you leaning toward? Keep this at the back of your mind. Especially if you're leaning toward America, your reasons to move have to be solid and strong.

2. **The American Struggle:** This is covered in detail later in the chapter, so I'll keep it short here. If you are struggling, can you try a location/job/friends/apartment change to see if that helps you first, instead of moving continents? I always lean on trying to make it work in America as much as mentally and physically possible.

3. **Why**: The saying goes 'When you find your why, you find a way to make it happen.' Your anchor is going to be your why.

- What is your anchor? Is it family, career, lifestyle, business, or something else?
- If it's family, do you want to live under the same ceiling or take the stairs up to their apartment or be a short rickshaw distance from them?
- If family is not an anchor, would you still want to move to India? No? Then think deeper about moving.
- For any anchor, think about how long it's going to ground or entertain you. If this is a weak link, please don't make any sudden decisions.

4. **Mitigation strategy**: Swiftly snap out a blank paper and scribble all the reasons you are afraid of moving to India. Afraid of being run over by a rickshaw, afraid of traveling backseat on a scooter – it could be anything. Then, brainstorm ways to mitigate these fears. For example, you hate the way your heart races when a truck drives close to you. Think of a mitigation. Can you get a driver? Can you take an Uber every day? Find out driver costs and Uber costs for some routes. Don't forget to check if it is affordable. Once you're done, at least you're aware of your fears and their mitigations. You will know what is in your hands to change, and what you're willing to sort of 'put up with.'

5. **Get real**: Visualize a life in India. Are you being realistic in your expectations of India? Reach out to a friend in India to validate these expectations.

6. **Reaching out to friends:** This is important as it helps give perspective.

- Make a list of 10 (yes 10, no less!) friends who can validate your hypothesis on mitigations and getting real.
- Your list should include women (not the wives of someone you just spoke to, as most spouses will give a similar outlook) and those living in different geographies.
- Get non-judgmental and mature people to give advice. Your question may look legitimate to you. "Can I get automatic hot water in apartments in India, instead of using a geyser?" If your friend is judgmental, I can see them rolling their eyes and telling their spouse, "Remember that NRI guy who called? Manish's friend? He asked if you get hot water in India. Haha, what a nutcase!"

7. **Magnitude change**: Return only when you are ready for something else to completely take priority in your life. Once you move to India, parts of your life will change drastically. For me, they were fitness and shopping, which have skydived into some Neverland that I can't find my way out of. What is your magnitude change going to be? The answer is that you can never predict what will change, but you can at least check if you're ready for a complete change.
8. **Visit/Live in India:** Visiting India frequently is a good idea. However, in subsequent parts of this chapter, I show you how it may not give a complete picture of life in India. This is mostly because moving to India is a commitment, not merely a like- or dislike-based decision.

Return only when you are ready for something else to completely take priority in your life.

9. **Gut feel**: It's important to see how you *feel*. If there is resistance from inside you, leave the thoughts in a small mental box and open it after a few years. If you are leaning toward India, you need to merely find the right time. We will explore this gut decision in a later part of this chapter.

10. **Time**: Gather facts around your immigration status. Do you need a re-entry permit? How many renewals remain on your H-1B? Talk to an immigration lawyer, your company will mostly have one, about possibilities and the repercussions of your status if you move. Find out what happens to your visa, social security, and taxes if you want to go to India for three months, six months, a year, or two years. I will explore more on the emotional side of time in Chapter Eight on Tipping Points.

11. **Patience**: Through this process, gulp down a dose of patience. The decision can be a long game. Even after moving, it takes a few years to redesign life in India, until you feel fully comfortable.

How to *not* Decide

Do You Fit In?

What if you move to India and, in five weeks, call up your friend and say, "*Yaar, feel ni aari* (Dude, I don't feel it)?"

You, the NRI, have limited means to figure out if India is for you before moving. You're probably tied down from exploring – by a visa, money, vacation limits, responsibilities, and the unchangeable constraint, which is distance. Your India is physically on the other side of the world. So you do what you can. While physically in America, you feel, think, and conclude about India – "Will I be able to make the same money, the same work-life balance, the same social circle? Will I be satisfied living in the place I grew up in?"

And then you conclude right there. When you are backing your car out of a remote-controlled garage and look at the MacBook lying on the heated leather seat next to you, an asset you can easily buy only because of your dollar income, you conclude: "Nope. India isn't the right move. Maybe later. But right now, I can deal with the discomfort of being away from India." Your confident conclusion is temporary because when you visit India, you oscillate again. You spiral back into confusion. 'I miss India. Can I move back?' The confusion is never cleared.

You might find it hard to 'fit in' in India. I still do! Every time you visit India, you don't remember how it got this way. When did the neighborhood shops get so crowded? Why isn't there a line at this bakery? You, in your shorts and floaters, look around, feeling alien and muse, "I don't think I can do this anymore. I don't fit in." This fearful conclusion is very real. The people density, selfie-takers in malls walking into you, the gloveless sugarcane vendor… you notice all of this and you assure yourself, "I guess I fit better in America."

Somehow, not *fitting in* still doesn't eliminate India for you.

India on vacation is painful to leave, especially for the NRI who is confused about moving to India. The thought of 'I don't think I can live here again' is followed by the resisting pain of 'I really want to give it a shot.' This oscillation between 'I can't do this' and 'I want to try' tires you out after many years. The confusion has been given assurance of 'don't worry, we'll eventually figure it out' so many times, that confusion becomes numb to procrastination. Postponing is, in a way, trying to ask the decision to make itself. The constant nagging needs to be laid to rest. You need ways to decide if the India move is the right thing to do.

Fear of Missing America Is Not a Good Way to Eliminate India

Fear that you're going to miss some things in America cannot be a reason to decide about moving to India.

What do you fear missing about America? The late-night dinners at Crepevine, driving at 65 mph, the chatting up a bus driver about the weather, the barre class which helped tone your arms? You will tell yourself, "I *am* going to miss this."

I thought I'd be missing something big – like my job, career, freedom, home, money, everything. In my last few days in America, I'd whisper to the beautiful San Francisco Bay Bridge, "I can't believe I am leaving you." By the evening, I'd look at the shiny restaurant lights on Mission Street and blurt out, "Oh shit, what am I doing." I wanted to kiss the clean sidewalks. I tried to stuff myself with chipotle burritos. I sat in my car and slid my sunroof up and down many times as if to get enough of it so that I can forget it later. I was supposed to miss all this.

But I don't. And instead, I miss weird things like omelets after a morning run and bitter breakfast lattes.

When I look back at what I thought I would miss, I laugh. It feels childish – as if India was going to be depriving me of experiences. As if what lay ahead of me was boring, depressing, and full of friction. As if I was going to leave a full life to go experience a sub-standard life.

I can say now what an injustice that is to India and its vast expanse of experiences and warmth. There are so many things to miss about America, and yet, so much makes up for it in India. For every guacamole I miss, I have authentic ***puneri vada pavs*** to make up for it. For every nacho I miss, there's a ***ghee dosa*** to make up for it.

The fear of missing America is greater than how much you will actually end up missing America. There is a book by Paul Coelho called *The Alchemist*, in which he says, famously, "The fear of suffering is worse than the suffering itself." This is important to know because you will spend more time consumed in worrying about what you're going to miss than actually missing it. There is, however, a fine print to this. If India is truly not for you, you'll miss America every day.

The fear of missing America is important to address. Like I mentioned before, list down your fears. It will reveal a lot about what may be truly important to you.

Simple actions or substitutes can mitigate your fears in India. Going to miss your bouncy bed and fluffy comforter? Ship it to India! Going to miss picking up Starbucks coffee? You might get woken up to freshly brewed Indian filter coffee. Going to miss the view from your tall French windows at home? You might instead have the ugly view of the neighbors ***baniyans*** through the grills on your balcony that you might choose to ignore when the voice of your aging father makes you smile. Who knows!

India is a state of mind. It has to be experienced. One cannot borrow answers from friends. The world of imagination and the real world are so different – the truth will surprise you. Take India as an adventure. Do not let 'missing America' stop you from moving.

Do You Really Need India or Do You Just Need a Break?

"I feel like I'm running at top speed on a treadmill that never stops."

– Me, alone in a foreign land.

Life in America is tough. Take a moment to pat yourself on the back for shouldering the stress. If you're earning an average income like I was, you cannot take a break from your work because the rent's gotta be paid. The vacation hours need to be saved for that 3-week trip to India. The job needs to be kept, even if you suffocate in it. The pain to keep working at all costs is omniscient in an immigrant's life. You can't see family for years, can't eat without worrying about costs, and you need to scratch your own damn back or pay $50 for a back massage. It's slow torture. You become restless and decide that you want to move to India. But is moving to India really the answer? Is your life a fast-moving, non-stop treadmill from which you need a break? Is your need for a break manifesting as a need to move back home?

It was a restless year for Swetha Shankar in Austin, TX in 2006. After staring for hours at a densely populated Word document, she decided she hated her job. She wanted to work with numbers, not documents! After getting rejected from, as she felt 'all Austin companies,' Swetha got impatient, fidgety, and restless. She'd had enough. She set a 4th July deadline that year to move to India. In her desperate need to get a job, she did everything possible through the Internet. She wrote begging emails to acquaintances in Gurgaon and sent 'I have strong experience in analytics' emails to Bangalore companies who never replied.

Swetha quickly dumped her plans by April. Maegan, a recruiter from Apple, called her. "Congrats! Your application has been approved after executive review!" Swetha grabbed the offer and was soon busy behind the tall glass walls in her new Apple office. She promptly forgot about moving to India.

A few years later, the intense feeling of moving to India came back. This was her fifth year in Austin, and she was bored of it. She said, "My friends moved to California, and the others? They got married and don't meet me anymore." Swetha was incredibly bored of Austin – the same commute, restaurants, and two left-over friends. The urge to move to India came back again. "I am sad every day, and I want to move to India." While she was applying to jobs in Bangalore, her transfer to the California HQ office was approved. On seeing the approval email, she pumped her hands in the air, made arrangements to move to California, and the urge to move to India dulled and receded, yet again.

As an NRI, do you also feel like Swetha? Perhaps some things are not working out for you – maybe you feel handcuffed to your job, feel suffocated from the H-1B stress, a boring boss, a mean roommate, or a breakup? Perhaps you are living in a small town in Michigan, or an airy apartment in Los Angeles, or a small closet-sized condo in New York and the urge to change grips and confuses you. It can mask as an urge to move to India.

When I hated my job, what I needed was a job change, not a location change. When I hated my location, I needed a small location change, perhaps not a big one. The time was not right to move to India during these needs. And when the time *was* right, ten years later, I even left my dream job to move to India.

Take my experience as a soft warning. Ask yourself if your craving for India is driven by a job that you can't find, a job that sucks, or a career that you can't fix.

This is not to say that your feelings for India are not genuine. It is just to say you should deeply consider a question – Am I loving India or am I hating my current situation?

Your Annual Visit Might Be Deceptive

The India you see during your yearly Thanksgiving vacation is not the India you will experience when you live in India.

NRIs experience India through the NRI filter during this annual trip. Digging into a crispy dosa at your old college hangout, pushing back the hands of your local friends who argue to pick up that bill, while pulling out your wallet for a lunch, you for once don't mind paying for. Sitting awkwardly with extended family in small living rooms, with all eyes on you, confessing to them about how you now present for your company at conferences, making them verbalize their innocent pride in your achievements (And they send the youngest man in the room to quickly buy a milk-based *mithai* to feed you) – all this is a visitor's India. It is loving, genuine, and exciting. For some, this dose of India is enough. Some want this excitement to go on forever. Because for a brief second, you are kissed with a sense of calm or happy.

After you move to India, your experience will be different from your annual visit experience. Your American status will linger on your sleeve for a few years and then fade away. The novelty of your being abroad will become passé, and people will treat you like one of their own – still curious, but much mellow-er. You will experience things differently. It might be a better India for you, actually. You no longer need to rush to stitch sari blouses. Hot masala chai comes to your work desk every single day. You want to try new food places as the old college hangout recedes into what it really is – an old college hangout with memories you have moved on from.

But why shouldn't your annual visit help you decide? Don't take this sitting down. You should be arguing with me. You should be jabbing your finger at news stories about the pollution in New Delhi, a problem that affects you during your annual visits, and you should be pulling my hand to sit me back down and tell me that this is real. Your experience of India is real. How can I deny that your visit to India isn't giving you a real experience of what your life in India will be like?

Of course, if your annual visit to India tells you that you don't really feel like moving, your mind has eliminated the possibility of moving. You're not confused anymore. The answer is staring at you in the face. Don't move.

But if your annual visit to India hasn't eliminated India, then you could still stretch it more with, what is called, a sabbatical. It is a short-but-long break that will allow you to take a few months off work.

Getting a feel in one visit or in a three-week immersion program or in a three-month sabbatical is hard to predict. If you can afford to, try visiting India multiple times over a period of 2-3 years. Stay with locals and do their chores with them. Offer to buy vegetables or fix the AC. Get a feel of how life will be for you, and this will reduce any shock or surprise when you move.

I wish companies had a separate immigrant vacation policy for employees whose families are not in the country. Taking one year off is a luxury few Indians can afford because of visa restrictions. So a vacation or sabbatical might be the only way to decide.

My extended three-month sabbatical in India was still deceptive in many ways. It did not have the *roz ka kich kich* that one faces in India. I traveled a lot, and the hotels I stayed in took care of water, electricity, and gas connection. They stopped rickshaws for me and arranged for a full-day driver and car support. It was comfortable, and I felt like a VIP. This kind of an arrangement is deceptive. It shields you from experiences that you will have when you really live in India – like the handling of the home rent, adjusting your time for the maid to come in, getting a gas connection renewed, or getting the cable guy to reset the TV channels. These add to your *roz ka kich kich*, which affects the quality of your daily life.

A sabbatical can still retain your doubts, which is okay, too, actually. After my sabbatical, there was one small progress. The sabbatical calmed me down a little, and I could say 'India is not, not for me.' A double negative. The sabbatical helped with the process of elimination rather than selection.

Even if you experience everyday Indian life in your visits, you cannot still understand India and its culture.

As a freshly returned NRI, I was gathering survey data in villages in the interiors of Madhya Pradesh, my colorful dupatta shielding my head from the strong sun. I spoke to a villager who was posed at the door of his home, the doorway framing his body.

"Do you get electricity?" I asked in Hindi and scribbled on my notepad.

"No," he said. Brief and to the point. Good.

But behind him, inside his small room, was a lone light bulb, and it was lit and shining. Of course, he had electricity!

"But that bulb is working. There is electricity," I quickly pointed with one end of my pen, expecting him to smack his head and say, "Duh, I forgot."

"No. We don't have electricity," he said without expression.

"Then, what's that?" I pointed again to the bulb, starting to find this ridiculous.

"That is private," he said.

"What?" My face scrunched up into a confused frown. 'Are you dumb?' I wanted to ask. He was saying he doesn't have electricity, while right there behind him was a shining bulb. If I had this conversation during my annual India visit, I would have dismissed him as a stupid villager and concluded I didn't want to live in India because people are stupid.

It was only later when I started understanding India that I realized the villager was technically correct. Hear me out. Due to some infrastructure issues, he had paid for a *private* electricity connection. (I assume he may have paid someone to steal electricity and wire it to his room). So yes, he didn't *get* electricity officially, but he *had* electricity. He had made it happen.

It was me who didn't know the right question to ask him, and it was me who didn't understand his language.

This local language can chew into your core initially. It certainly annoyed me. Perhaps you might be annoyed by something else during your sabbatical, and you might make decisions on wrong parameters.

All I'm saying is this: Though a vacation or sabbatical in India might help bring you closer to your decision, be careful in judging your future life from a few weeks of visiting. The decision to move to India is more of a 'No matter what, this is the right thing for me at this time' kind of resolve. Don't hold India up to the expectations of your annual visit, as you might be disappointed later. This extends to everything in life – hopes and disappointments go hand in hand.

Deciding Through the Eyes of Friends

Rohit Roy was an NRI who lived in the Richmond area of Seattle. In his desperation to figure out if he should move to India, he would question anyone who was brown-skinned and looking unhappy.

"Would you live in Bangalore?" he'd ask them.

One NRI friend answered, "I don't want to move. I would have to live in a gated community, which feels just like America."

Rohit then spoke to a friend who had just moved to India. He said, "I don't miss America. I live in a gated community, which feels just like America!"

Same housing. Different feelings. One hating it, one pleased with it. Rohit didn't know who to believe.

Rohit's quest to find an answer continued. His worry was the Bangalore traffic, and these were the inputs he heard:

"Bangalore traffic is the worst," said an NRI friend who had visited Bangalore once.

"Bangalore? I would never move there; I heard the traffic is terrible," another NRI friend said.

"Bangalore, huh? Stay next to the office," suggested a Bangalore employee.

"Bangalore!! Oh man, like once, I like landed at like 9 AM at the Bangalore airport. And guess when I like reached my hotel?" a young colleague told him.

Rohit deliberately kept his guesses low so that his surprise looked like real surprise. "Hmm, in one hour?"

"Dude, no! Like 12:30 PM. Can you believe it? Like three plus hours! Traffic was like bad!"

When Rohit finally moved to Bangalore, he expected to be putting his head out from his car window and yelling, "*Saale! Andha hai kya?* (Stupid, are you blind?)" to pedestrians and fist-punching other drivers. He was expecting to be bored while stuck in traffic, reading 'horn ok please' signs on the back of trucks. He was prepared to stock up on books to consume in his chauffeur-driven car.

But after 10 months in Bangalore, Rohit had no such experiences. The trip to office took him 40 minutes, and the time melted away in conversation. He'd either call his family or talk to his carpool cab mates about varied topics – work, home, and the traffic. Yes, he was parked on the road often, but he modified his meeting times accordingly. There wasn't any fear of living outside the *Lakshman rekha* of office. Rohit would have never predicted this. He was never able to put a price on the advice given by friends. Was he an anomaly or was he made of a different temperament than them, that his experiences and feelings were so different from theirs?

Be careful. In asking questions to your friends, are you looking for an answer that is in resonance with your feelings? Do you find comfort in hearing 'Yes, I hated living in India, so I am coming back'?

Such inputs could be a confirmation of your deepest fears. You might be seeking or remembering answers that you want to hear.

Asking friends if their move was successful is also not a good way to decide. Asking someone 'You've moved to India; is it better for you now?' is like asking if the weather is better. It's not the right metric. The weather may be good today and poor tomorrow, much like our moods. You have to experience India for yourself.

Learning from Rohit, I encourage you to be fluid in your decisions and take friends' advice with a pinch of salt. Human nature is to complain. When everything is going smoothly, nothing is said. Twitter feeds of companies' social media accounts are littered with the eruptive lava of abusive words of customers who had a bad experience – praise is rarely expressed.

Your Friends Won't Give You the Right Reason

Are you sure your friends are telling you the truth? I'll let you in on a secret: many NRIs don't give you the real reason why they moved to India. Meet Payal Patel, a QA analyst who's moved from NJ with her husband, Preetam. When she meets you at a catch-up dinner in Hyderabad, she'll say that they moved to India to turn Preetam's unicorn idea into a startup.

What she can't tell you is that the move actually happened because Preetam had a run-in with his manager. They almost fired him, and he was struggling to find another job in time. He hurriedly packed up to move to India. She also can't tell you how badly he and Payal fought: He threw the car keys across the floor, she ran into her bedroom to bury her crying face into a pillow, while their two-year-old child slept in a crib.

You'll never know.

And you don't need to know.

Because your reason, feeling, and experience are entirely yours. Your experience will change depending on your phase of life, age, gender, children, living parents, or a recently deceased parent.

You can listen to your friends about their experiences in India. But remember your friends' reasons may not apply to your situation. They might not be able to reveal everything that you need to know to make a decision. They have the best intentions but they also have a different lens. They are not you.

Gut Feeling: Is India for Me Right Now?

What if everything looks good on paper and your mental spreadsheet checks all the boxes? Job? Check.

Location? Check.

Sabbatical? Check.

Asking strangers? Check.

Yet, moving to India still does not feel right, and you can't pin it down.

What could it possibly be?

Perhaps a better question to ask yourself is this: Is India for me right now? There might be a lingering feeling inside you that your time hasn't come yet.

This unsettling feeling comes out in two forms – one of them is FOMO (Fear of Missing Out). It is a stomach-freezing feeling that something important is coming up in the future. If you leave America, you will miss out on some opportunity.

I had this FOMO feeling repackaged in the feeling that I hadn't 'taken the juice out of America just yet.' There was an unseen list to explore, after the visible list of national parks, big cities, road trips, future friends, and a husband. Though some of these didn't happen to me, not due to lack of trying, my intuition turned out to be right. I did have other big opportunities come my way. They were of discovering my inner talents – these were priceless discoveries and you're reading the result of one of them.

The feeling that the time is not right has some weightage, and you need to listen to it carefully. I listened to that feeling of FOMO and was able to park my move to India aside – *not now.*

The second sign that your time to move has not come is slightly spiritual-based. You tried so hard, and nothing is working out. God works in strange ways, and if you're still not lifting off that foreign land, it might be a sign that your time hasn't come now.

There is a third sign that the time is not right, and that is when your will is not strong enough. Judge yourself by what you do and not what you say. Did you tank your plan to move after you got a girlfriend? Then this might not be the right time. But then when is the right time? We will explore more in Chapter Eight, which talks about when this move happens.

Justifying Your Own Non-Action

A healthy society will raise a toast to a successful person. They will kiss his cheeks and buy him a reasonable dinner at PF Changs.

But a dissatisfied society will cringe from his success and love his failures. The question is this: Is the NRI Diaspora a healthy society?

After I moved to India, I encountered a distributed set of NRIs, who were like vultures preying on a dying animal. They were waiting for even one answer from me that would announce a hint of failure. Under the guise of curiosity, they'd ask me, "How's it going?" A few weeks later, "So, how's it going *now*?" Then, a few more weeks later, "How about *now*?" I've been showered with opinions: "You're not even getting a good salary there." They dictate in many different words: "You should come back." I couldn't help notice the pattern – curiosity followed by condescending comments. When I expressed anything negative about my Indian life, something as mundane as 'The service provider canceled on me,' they had a strong reaction: "See. This is why. This is why I am not moving to India."

I recognized one day that this curiosity was coming from a wish – their wish to see me fail.

They wanted to prove that their decision to *not* move to India was correct, by showing me that my decision to move to India was wrong. It is deep down, a hollowness, a dark feeling. Perhaps they don't know it themselves because they couldn't bring up the courage to do what they wanted and so are looking at signs of any failure to justify their non-action. And since I saw these dark clouds, I've had to downgrade these friends to acquaintances; some even got priority slots on the rare 'blocked list.'

The question is this: Are you one of them, justifying your non-action to yourself?

This Is a Hard Decision

Anonymous comments on various websites have revealed what the world thinks: 'If you Indians love India, why don't you go back to your country?'

I could be accused of thinking that too. A girl I knew in California cried over dinner with me and described, in a teary monologue, her terrible life in America where she had no status. She'd left a life in India where she had a reputed job. She hated her job in America where she had to merely track statuses of online tickets. And I wondered, as she wiped her tears with the sleeves of her t-shirt, why she didn't just go back.

The question itself is wrong. It's not about 'why don't you just leave?' It's about 'what is preventing you from leaving?' Are NRIs a failure because they want to go to India and aren't able to make it happen?

If that were true, then is my divorced friend who can't move to India because the law does not allow her to leave her son a failure? There are NRIs who cannot move even if there is death in the family. The reason of 'my mother is alone, I need to move back to India' has also not proved to be enough to make NRIs act. We think it's *easy* to move, but it's not.

This is a hard decision. Give yourself some slack if you're worried about it. It *is* worthy of worrying. It's okay. You've got this.

8

WHEN WILL YOU MOVE? THE TIPPING POINT

2 Dec 2006, 00:46
Atlanta, Georgia
Hey Ashish,

Do you think I could try applying in your company? I'm looking to move to India in 2-3 years, so I thought I'll move to California to experience life there for a bit before I move.

Let me know your thoughts! I've attached my resume.

Thanks,
Nupur

I found this (verbatim) email that I had sent in 2006, where I expressed my intention to move to India in 2-3 years. I had no idea it would take me 10 years to make it happen. My inbox is littered with such nuggets of intermittent urges to move back. The emails now make me laugh and smack my head. Slowly, when the laughter dies down and I think about how I felt then, these emails make me sigh. The intention to move and the act of moving were separated by 10 years of confusion, introspection, experimentation, and finally, a tipping point.

We've heard plenty of 'I will try to move to India next year' statements. We've heard an equal number of postponements to an unspecified later period: "Actually, Shalini just joined Cisco na, so we won't go this year." Youngsters who move to America are confident they will return in a few years. With a naivety that sounds cute, they say, "I just want to move to America to make money and then move back to India in two years."

Clearly, it's a difficult decision to make for everyone, so ease up on yourself. Most moving-to-India statements are merely intentions. Intention doesn't mean action. For me, the time difference between intention and action was 10 years, but the time difference between decision and action was a few months. **Most Moving-to-India Statements Are Merely Intentions. Intention Doesn't Mean Action**

Once you know you want to move, when will you turn that intention into action? That is the million-dollar question. We often say, "It's not a matter of *if* I am moving, it's a matter of *when*." There is no clear answer to 'When?' Let's use our proverbial binoculars to look at the different types of tipping points that have happened to others.

1. **Organic tipping point**

"You can live one year over and over again five times, or live five years once."

– Unknown

Sheetal Soni's H-1B life, as a financial analyst in Chicago, was on a boring auto-repeat. Despite that, and the frequent urge to go back to her Mumbai home, she still felt no compelling reason to make a move to India. There was no tipping point.

Sheetal's life was repeating the same Ajanta clock tune. Every year, she would hesitate to renew her lease in the hope of marriage. Every year, she'd be going through the same problem of finding a new roommate and then arguing over who would take the master bedroom. Every year, she'd exhaust her paltry 15 leaves for an India trip. The fleeting but familiar feelings would repeat – not wanting to leave America while at the Chicago airport and not wanting to leave India while at the Mumbai airport.

Every year, her friends at housewarming parties would say, "You should buy a home too, Sheetal," She'd swipe a hand in the air and reply, "Doubt it. I won't be able to move back to India then."

Sheetal's problems never went away, and the routine got her bored. The boredom got her sad. Every year, it was the same rental problems – The same traffic on a different road, the same financial problems, the same craving for companionship, the same December trip to India, and the same 'I love my country' feeling. This life was cyclical, and these irritants came predictably like the monsoons – a few weeks off here and there, but they appeared. The pressure in her cooker of feelings would increase a bit every time she woke up to this immigrant life. Moving was a decision always postponed as her immediate future always had something to look forward to – a fast-moving work pace, office parties, a conference, an offsite, or opportunities to travel.

Until one day, the pressure cooker burst.

Sheetal had in her hand an offer from a consulting firm on Millennial Drive, where she'd be a senior manager but something didn't feel right. She met her friend Rebecca, a wise lady in her fifties, who told her, "Sheetal, you can live one year five times, or you can live five years at once. You decide. You decide if you want to live the same life over and over again with the same problems over and over again, or change something, and live a full life. "

Sheetal stepped back and looked at her life. If she took up this job, she was committing to another few years of living the same life again in the hope that something would change for her. "Enough!" she felt. This is how life presented it for Sheetal.

Tipping points that bubble up organically and push you into the boxing ring of decision making could come for you, or never come. The triggers to an organic tipping point are not in your hands. It could be your child's age, your own age, being bored or lonely, or being simply tired of living the same life again and again that makes you decide enough is enough. Life pushes you to make the decision.

Tipping points that bubble up organically and push you into the boxing ring of decision making could come for you, or never come. Make the most of them.

2. **Event-based tipping point**

Event-based moves happen when a circumstance presents itself, which compels you to move. It is difficult to predict an event-based move. They could be visa issues, getting fired, parents getting admitted to hospital, a death in the family, or something specific like 'My brother is moving to America, so I have to move to my hometown.' There isn't much you could have done here. You need to be aware that many moves to India are triggered by such events.

Notice, I didn't put in the list of events the conch calling for a new career. Is a job opportunity an event-based tipping point?

Manas Mehta, from NYC, was approached to become the CTO at a Bangalore startup. He moved to take up a unique career opportunity – proximity to parents was a byproduct. Moving to India for a job opportunity sounds like an event-based move, but I would argue this is not 'Return to India' but merely a geo-relocation for a career opportunity.

3. **Deadline-based tipping point**

You can create your own tipping point deadline to move to India.

"I picked a random date of December 15th, and we decided to move, no matter what," mentions Mithila Menon from Hyderabad. This is a method similar to jumping directly into the rivers to learn swimming. It's fun for some, terrifying for others.

There could possibly be one way to make a tipping point happen for yourself – Completely isolate yourself from the world for a few days. A 10-day course of silence and meditation has known to bring out core feelings. Why 10 days? Anything shorter doesn't give you enough time to calm the chatter in your mind. Many people have found clarity on life decisions after an extended silent retreat because their true feelings bubble up. I firmly believe your body intuitively knows if the time is right or not. You just have to listen to it.

What if you feel the time is right, but your dependents don't feel so? One way to deal with it would be to put a longish 1-2 year deadline on moving, and watch your feelings till the deadline. Do your feelings change? Do you remember your deadline every day?

As you can see from each of these tipping points, it's hard to know what will work for you. We cannot predict when your tipping point will come or what will push you over the edge. In the end, it's a combination of destiny and will and timing. And even after you decide, you may have one more hurdle to cross – salary.

Salary Gets in the Way of Moving

If you're ready to dive into the deep end, it might be useful to know that salary is the number one reason to abort a move.

NRIs returning to India are thrown out of their socks by the shock of the salary reality – the shock that you might have to move despite your salary, and sadly, not because of it.

My friend Sukhwani Singh, a young product manager in California, called to inform me that she had aborted her move to India.

"The companies are paying too little, yaar," her confident but disappointed voice told me over the phone.

I asked her what less meant. It turned out to be 35 LPA. I coolly agreed, pretending that 35 LPA was indeed an appallingly low number! *How dare they!* All the while, I was squeezing the life out of a squishy stress ball in my fist. How could I tell her I was earning way less than that?

Sukhwani was expecting 40 LPA or more. I don't know how much Sukhwani should earn, but I do know that product managers at her age and years of experience drew salaries in the range from 18-26 LPA.

Why do NRIs have expectations that do not match with market standards?

One, some numbers come from anecdotal salaries: – My client's wife negotiated a 75 LPA, a house and a car... and a cat.

Two, there is always someone in that sample size of the friends you speak to who should and will be earning more than you.

Three, when we hear of 60 lakh or one crore salaries, it anchors a number into our heads and we think that we'll get 40-50 LPA easily. I really do wish you get this kind of salary, though meanwhile, do consider why you command that salary for reasons other than being a US return.

There seems to be a $1/3^{rd}$ rule floating around – One should be offered $1/3^{rd}$ of their US salary in India. Someone who wants to stay anonymous tells me the range is 1/2 to $1/5^{th}$. So it could be statistically possible that your salary falls in that $1/3^{rd}$ range. It's difficult to confirm you'll get that. Or more. Or less.

So what is a good salary? How much money is enough? The answer is that no amount of money is enough. Money is, by nature, never enough. But the truth is that you don't need much money to survive in India.

Indian salaries sound like a step-down – a salary of 25 LPA, which when laid out in bare is ₹25,00,000 or in American greens, is *only* $35,000 per year. This is a great number if you have a particular lifestyle and inadequate if you have another.

No amount of money is enough. Money is, by nature, never enough. But the truth is that you don't need much money to survive in India.

What would I do with your 25 LPA? With 12% of that monthly income, I will pay my rent of ₹25,000. Then I'll pay ₹7000 to my maid and ₹5000 to a gym that I might not visit. My veggies? I have no idea what it costs me because I assume the maid will buy it. So I ballpark ₹4000 for veggies and a generous ₹5000 for entertainment. Another ₹5000 on clothes and ₹10,000 on travel. Total spend? ₹61,000. I still save about a lakh a month. That's a lot of money to play with. But If I live like a princess, I could spend all that income just on my rent!

Answer for yourself – what do you *need* for the lifestyle you wish to have?

Unrealistic Expectations of What India Is Like

Do you fancy yourself enjoying the cold Himalayan air while hanging out of a truck, singing *phataka guddi* with your hair flying in the wind? Are you hoping that when you move to India, you will suddenly be elevated from your database admin job in America to a manager of 100 people? Are you dreaming your India job will make you hear 'Ma'am, I printed your First Class tickets to the conference in London. You'll be staying at the Ritz'? Are you hoping you'll be able to renovate your current home into an architecture digest home with glass ceilings, without interaction with the vendors?

These are unrealistic expectations, simply because they are outcomes independent of what goes into getting to them. The dream of living in an architecture digest-worthy home requires a lot of money, and you will have to interact with vendors who might not be within your professional expectations. If you're currently a level-three individual contributor, remember that the management landscape in India is pretty cut-throat. You have to be offering something more than an entry-level value addition for employers to pay you big bucks. I have seen many instances of people hoping or assuming that they will get magnitudes of elevation in their designation in India. It is better to instead work toward such a dream eventually, instead of moving to India with a perception that you will be automatically elevated.

It's advisable to be realistic in your self-assessment and choose a job accordingly. In my case, I know my skin is not made of Teflon – heck, I am a writer. I am overflowing with emotions. Can I be Steve Jobs? No. Can I be the one to handle a boardroom full of egos? No. Can I handle scheming people? No. So I will choose a company where they want people like me. Is that easy to find? No!

Your realism about what India can offer you will change your experience. If you come with an open mind, untainted by what you think you deserve, and see how things unfold, it would be a smoother transition.

Finding a Job in India

When an NRI decides to move, the panic of 'needing a job *right now*' overcomes them. Many NRIs have martyred their resumes in hurriedly submitted job applications. Like in any part of the world, job applications need the wand of strategy and a pinch of patience.

The first obvious question is this: Will I get a job in India from America itself?

The only reasonable answer to this is that it depends.

If your profile and luck are strong, you might get an offer while in America. If you don't get one, don't let it puncture your confidence. The NRI survey shows that more than 50% of NRIs (might include spouses) move to India without a job in hand. Being physically present in India with an Indian address is the next best thing to increase the probability of being hired.

Moving to India is a huge shift for anyone. I recommend not changing too many parameters when you move. The most optimal way to move is with your current company. Sumit Gwalani confirms this. Sumit moved from Google California to Google India in 2013 and co-founded Google Pay. He's now co-founder at a startup, Epifi. He advises: "India can be a hard landing. Find a job where you're familiar with the culture. The best option is to transfer through your current company. The next best is an MNC with an established culture or a new-age startup. For couples, even if one spouse does that, it will help them settle and ease into non-work challenges."

When moving to India, I recommend not changing too many parameters when you move. The most optimal way to move is with your current company.

If you're thinking that you will move only if you get a good job offer, we need to talk about the compromises someone would have to make to move past this point. Salary, job content, and timing – perhaps not all come together at the same time. You can proceed with a lower salary and then re-interview for a better job.

NRIs have a few myths and misconceptions in the job-hunting world. Some prominent myths are:

1. "I have a foreign degree. That should help." Not really, I'm afraid.
2. "I am an NRI, so I should get a higher salary." Again, not really. A recruiter who wishes to stay anonymous finds NRIs annoying because "…they seem to expect ridiculous salaries and come with a sense of entitlement." I don't have any experience concerning that statement, but I think it's an insight definitely worth sharing.

3. "I have a US citizenship. That will be an advantage to the company because I can travel to the US easily." Surprisingly, no.

4. "I will be the best applicant for all job profiles." Another recruiter who wishes to stay anonymous says, "NRIs may have a disadvantage in jobs that require a lot of local hustle. Like, say, account management with local clients. Some companies prefer a local who is familiar with navigating the culture and won't put an NRI fresh off the seas into a job like that."

However, there are advantages to being an NRI in the job market. Anand Rangarajan, the engineering head of Google Bangalore, speaks to me about some advantages of hiring NRIs. "You can expect they have greater exposure to global culture. A better understanding of how to communicate. Additionally, (there is a hypothesis that) NRIs who become managers have a much lower chance of turning out to be micromanagers."

Watch out for the potentially scarring and varied experiences while finding a job. The front-line to hiring are recruiters. Through them, you may find a distinctly different and possibly jarring introduction to recruiting in India. I've been shocked by questions put to me: "Are you single?" "How soon do you plan to marry?"

Later, I learned the marriage of single women is a concern for many companies. Most women relocate or leave their jobs when they marry, and HR would like to know.

You may see a range of recruiters: amazing, empathetic recruiters or recruiters untrained to distinguish between a fresher and an experienced person. The latter often talk like they are doing you a favor by giving you a job – 'Tell me your salary expectations. Otherwise, we can't tell if we can hire you or not!' This usually happens if your referral comes from someone who isn't in senior management. Such front-line conversations spoil the flavor of a company. I would suggest to not take such experiences as a predictor of how you would feel in India or in the company.

Your interviews may also cover a range of experiences. I have been interviewed by incredibly humble and smart people who use professional conversations to judge you. I have also been interviewed by immature youngsters who want to have fun, evident from their body language – leaning back into the chair, staring at you, and occasionally 'heh'ing an answer or expecting a 'right answer' to the question. They are judging you with a yardstick you don't want to bother measuring up to. I looked around their office, and it was clear that they hired people who mirror them. I would also urge you to meet people in person. Visiting offices and feeling the energies can help you decide or eliminate faster.

There is overwhelming proof that job search is a painful experience all over the world. If your job search is not coming along well, before you get angry at India, realize that frustration is in the nature of job search.

9

ADJUSTING IN INDIA

Introduction to Adjusting in India

Now you've moved to India and post the move, your life is filled with comparisons with your American life. For some NRIs, this comparison comes with a flavor of bias – the assumption that America is *better* than India. This NRI will tilt his head past the front seat of the taxi and tell his parents in the back seat, "In America, they have cameras at every signal, and breaking a signal makes you automatically get a traffic violation." As if the parents don't know. He will want to call for the manager of the supermarket to suggest: "Why don't you make a single line for checkout? That's how they do it abroad." He will pick up the rupee price tag of a BIBA salwar in a store, convert the numbers out loud, and state: "That's about 40 dollars. Not bad at all!"

Why will comparing life in America to life in India work against you?

A comparison of your life has two repercussions.

One, it might frustrate you, making it harder to settle in. There will be more struggles inside your mind than in the outside world.

Two, when you verbalize your comparison, it irritates people around. No one wants to hear comparisons along the lines of 'You Indians can't even....'

You have got to let go of expectations from India and work toward understanding India because in this lies your happiness. So how do you get past comparison and settle in? This is where you need a strategy to design your life in India.

It took me one and a half years to fully settle into my own country – let that sink in. You may have lived in America for a few years or long enough to return with a calibrated American accent.

In both cases, without a strategy to settle, you might have a mentally turbulent transition and make monetarily costly mistakes.

I have an equation that you could ponder on. It's easy to remember but hard to implement. It's called the three A's – *Accept, Adapt,* and *Adopt.*

Accept Things That Won't Change

It was my first month in India, and I could only see my own feet because I was sandwiched in the office elevator, between five women and one man. I was measuring the back of the short man's head when the elevator stopped, and he did the unimaginable.

Had this been America, he would have swept a hand to hold the elevator door and let the ladies go out first. But no, he stepped out first. He plucked himself out of the elevator and confidently moved forward, like a defiant man leaving his lovers behind. I was so angry – *Women are supposed to get out first!* On paper, it sounds like he made a small misdemeanor, but when it played out in front of my freshly returned NRI eyes, it looked like a felony! I wanted to reach my hand out in slow motion, hook my index finger into the rim of his t-shirt, and pull him back, glaring my almond eyes at him. I wanted to shout into his bespectacled face: "Ladies first!" It should have taught him a good lesson to let women through doors first.

Like they do in America.

I was so used to it. Men in America did the one-hand door sweep to let a woman pass through. Every man does it – known, unknown, rich, poor, and famous men – you as a woman are always the first ones to pass.

But in India, opening doors is not a part of the local culture. Here, people confidently walk through a door and release it instantly, unintentionally slamming the door in your face if you're right behind. I tried to teach by example, often leaning my arm over a door in the office. The result, a stream of people simply walked past me. I was expecting in return of my smart, magnanimous generosity a head turn or a quick nod or any acknowledgment of my action – there was none.

It upset me. *This is basic courtesy*, I thought. Every time I saved myself from a door slamming into my face, I'd remember how it was in America. All these door openings were moments of 'that escalated quickly,' where I went from *I'm hungry, let's get lunch* to *Did I really need to move back to India?!*

It bothered me immensely for a whole of three months. Every single time a door slammed into my face, anger would bubble up inside me and subside in many minutes. With countless, distressed door insults over time, I started to get used to it, and my anger turned into acceptance. The door-opening culture dropped from my rotating radar of morality.

Now, I have stopped questioning the your-door-you-open culture. It's one of those nice to have's. I no longer feel the need to upturn a desk, shout into a megaphone, and put up banners for a revolution called the 'Damn Door Openers Club.' I have tuned my hands to quickly stop a swinging door from slamming over my surprised face, but I continue to keep the door open for people behind me. With my acceptance, my anger's gone, and I've calmed down.

Acceptance really helped me settle in India. I accepted that riders in Pune don't wear a helmet. I focused on other impactful changes that I could make, such as to keep wearing a helmet myself. I accepted that people do bargain with poor vendors for vegetables, and at least I could continue to pay the asked price without argument.

I accepted that culturally people don't thank drivers, but I continued to do so even if the driver won't respond.

I am still struggling with accepting one reality. I mentioned before that buildings and apartments in India are not standardized, unlike America. You are familiar with the American standards – public doors with horizontal bars at waist height, apartments with clean white bathtubs, and restrooms stalls that come up to your shins. In India, I've worked in upscale offices. I've also worked in cheap offices where the sink is rusty, a rat visits at night, and I've shooed *kabootars* (pigeons) from the office restroom. I have not dropped my expectations about how companies should spend their money in terms of office space. I withdraw inside every time I visit offices that scream 'Let's make do with the cheapest option,' and I have to stop myself from voicing it.

ADOPT and ADJUST: Take up Local Rules

There were many things you, as a freshly returned NRI, will do the American way in your first months in India. During your taxi travels, you might argue with the driver about a non-functional rear seatbelt. In defiant fear of your safety, you might wrap the limp non-functioning seat belts around your arm – the type of behavior that drivers may roll their eyes to. You might pull down your taxi window and point out to bike riders, requesting them to please wear a helmet. You might question why all hotels are called Om Sai Palace and will ask for 'water, no ice' in restaurants.

You will continue your American ways, till you get enough empirical data to understand why the world around you isn't changing. You're exhausting yourself fighting with a system that you don't understand. You are pushing your limits to achieve a perception of how you think India should be.

So you might have to adopt. Adopt the local method of not wearing a seatbelt on the rear seat, when empirical data proves you're always at less than 20 mph. Adopt the local practice of talking to the mechanic or delivery boy only if needed. Like I did when I saw that culturally, the man on the street isn't comfortable with an effervescent woman asking '*ghar pe kaun-kaun hai?* (who's in your family?)' He felt more comfortable if instead a man asked him *ghar pe kaun-kaun hai.*

Cultural understanding and acceptance is key to your smooth transition. When you hear anecdotes of bad experiences from your friends, you would never choose to move to India, out of fear – How will I handle these situations? But what you need to believe is that when you do move, you *will* adapt, adopt, and accept. You *will* learn. You *will* know when to let it go.

> **But what you need to believe is that when you do move, you *will* adapt, adopt, and accept. You *will* learn.**

Adjusting to the 'You Have to Know' Culture

It is conversationally acceptable in India to be non-exact in what you say. The expectation is that the listener has to understand – *Bhavnao ko samjho* (Understand the feelings behind my words). The non-exactness of information can be unsettling and confusing to a freshly moved NRI. If someone says '*Mujhe thyroid hai* (I have thyroid),' you have to understand that the statement is not a mere acknowledgment of the existence of their thyroid gland, but it probably means they have Hypothyroidism.

For maybe a year, I was irritated with vaguely put forward information. I have a favorite non-exactness, which is *normal.*

Me: "What time do you usually come to office?"

Colleague: "Normal time."

Me (spoon hovering over a teacup): "How much sugar in the tea?"

Friend: "Normal!"

Me: "How much milk in the tea?"

Friend: "*Wohi...* Normal…"

My favorite was an overheard conversation:

Gym Instructor: "Are you right-handed or left-handed?"

Client: "Hain? Normal!"

During the tea-milk exchange, I wanted to scream 'AAARGH!' I almost verbalized, "Tell me exactly how much sugar you want, or give me a range I can work with."

Understanding this language takes time, just like how I couldn't get the villager and his electricity. After years of serving sugar, milk, and asking questions, I got an idea of what normal means. Normal time for office is 10 AM, normal sugar is one spoon, and normal milk is whatever you find appropriate. Maybe people frame it this way, so that they don't look too picky, because too picky could be annoying too.

Non-exactness extends to feedback as well. It's normal to describe any experience as '*accha*' (good). **You have to know to read between the lines to really make something of an answer.**

Me: "How was the movie?"

Friend: "*Accha tha*!"

Me: "Did you like the character?"

Friend: "Yes. *Accha tha*"

The mood continues:

Employee: "How is my performance?"

Manager: "*Accha hai*"

Obviously, this is described in jest. It may not be common in your experience. And don't you dare mistake this for stupidity. People might not be comfortable opening up their opinions to you or might be intricately descriptive in their mother tongue.

A common problem I've faced is when people can't say no. For example, you want to talk to a friend about borrowing their vacuum cleaner. You'll tell them, "Can I call you at eight to discuss the logistics?" If the friend isn't comfortable lending their vacuum cleaner, they might say, "Yes, call me!" and simply not pick up your phone. You have to just know that they don't want to talk to you. There is no, "Sorry, I'm not comfortable lending my stuff." There is only reading between the lines. It comes with practice.

India still runs on verbal recommendations. You've got to 'know' what people mean. You also got to 'know' how to *do* things. Seasoned NRIs make rookie mistakes in India – like using online reviews to judge services. My favorite beauty parlor, run by Veena Aunty, has mediocre reviews online. I picked her after multiple bad experiences at other places. You will tell me, "Okay, forget online reviews. I will pick the most expensive parlors." Sure, but this is the number one pet peeve that visitors have about India – more money doesn't guarantee excellent service. The expensive *Le French* parlor doesn't mean they'll do a more majestic manicure than Veena Aunty's parlor. This culture of 'you gotta know' can be learned only over time.

Adjusting by Not Looking for America in India

The NRI assumes he'll have the same American experiences in India. He'd like to pass his hands over brinjal in the supermarket. At the checkout counter, he'll greet the scanning lady with 'heyhowreya' in one breath and one-hand swivel his car out of the parking spot after loading his car with his groceries.

When you expect this American life in India, you face an oddity – What if you can't have it? What would you do?

"I don't think I'll hire a maid when I move," an NRI once told me.

"Why?"

"I don't eat much. I'll fix myself a salad every day."

Every time an NRI says 'I will move to India and make salads every day' I cringe a little. It's not about the salad (or salaad as we call it in India). It's about the expectation to recreate the same American life. If you must, really, you will find a way to recreate it. It's not going to be easy. What if you don't get fresh vegetables? What will you do when you can't get your arugula leaves, kale, and caramelized walnuts? What if you're not happy with the type of salad leaves? What will you do?

You can throw money at the problem, but often, money doesn't guarantee service. The upkeep of an American lifestyle is possible for sure – it just costs a lot of money.

Keep your expectations in check, an open mind, and do not insist on recreating America in India for you will be sad and disappointed.

Newly returned NRIs may also stand out because they are still in their habits of the past. The newly returned NRI is saying hello to elevator operators. She's asking 'how was your weekend' to unprepared co-workers, lathering her hands with Purell before a meal, and asking for the 'restroom.' Nothing wrong with that! It's just different. You stand out. People notice. Nothing wrong with that either. This behavior might look eccentric. The difference is that Americans appreciate eccentricity. Indians remember eccentricity. The question you want to dwell on is this: Do you want to move on from America and adopt some local cultural traits, or do you want to stay the same? I have no answer to this – it's up to you.

Adjust to a Judgmental Society

One issue in your list of fears, circled in red ink, is Indian inquisitiveness: Will society in India bother me? Will uncles on the opposite couch, with chai in hand, ask you, "So beta, what is your salary?" Will the neighbors linger in their balconies and lean back to look into your living room when you have friends of the other gender over? Will your relatives gasp in shock when you tell them you are not a manager in office? Will they 'tch tch' you if they find out you're single or a divorcee? Will they nudge the side of your ribs and eye-point to a cute girl and tell you that you should be interested?

I would say that this fear of being judged has nothing to do with where you live. You may have left India, but you will find Indian society even in America. I've been told offensive and intrusive statements by the Indian diaspora in America! The usual 'You've put on weight.' The judgmental 'I thought you were interested in the guy you were talking to, wink wink.' The lecturing 'Just find a nice guy and get married, na.' I have heard these sweet judgments while in America! The point being, you should not stop your move to India, because you think society is going to ask you questions.

You cannot predict how society will react to you. In India, society's reactions are oscillating between extremes. People might smile and leave you alone or can ask you questions on your looks, weight, status, or job. You can never predict it.

Society is still asking questions, perhaps not directly. If a neighbor wants to know who the new guy in his neighborhood is, he will ask your watchman for details. "He's come from America. Works as a software engineer." Satisfied, the neighbor will smile at you or leave you alone. In the office, observers will elbow their friends in your team, and ask, "Who's the new guy?" Your own team might find their information-elixir in a friendly conversation with you, or never ask you personal details at all.

You will soon learn to navigate society and learn to put boundaries around you.

If your uncle asks you about your salary, you will learn to dilute your answer. If your gym friend comments on your hips, you will learn to smile and joke about it. If a neighbor forces you to get a job for his son, you'll learn to diplomatically say no. Give it time, because time is a price you have to pay.

The Cost of Settling Down

Adapting to India after many years abroad doesn't come cheap. You will make mistakes after moving to India. You will make monetary mistakes – pay double because you got confused between *pachas* (50) and *pacchis* (25). You will make cultural mistakes – maybe you will point out a spot on the floor to the sweeper and say, "That part is left out." And he may react to you as if you were accusing him of not doing his job, while you were merely helping him finish. You will make trusting mistakes – falling for sweet talks of rogue friends who say they will reach in five minutes, and you end up waiting for an hour.

Every new day, you will learn a new stupidity in you. But you will learn. Iteratively, till it smooths out. Make a mistake. Learn. Make a mistake. Learn.

The most valuable advice I got for settling into India was from a friend, Rahul, who has a Ph.D. in economics, though his advice has nothing to do with his Ph.D. He says, "Keep a budget for mistakes. You may have to spend extra money because you don't know how things work in India. You may have to pay a higher price because you look, behave, and talk like an outsider. Give yourself space to learn these lessons. Give it a year."

Rahul calls it the cost of settling down.

For me, the cost of settling down was high initially before it cliff-dived. I spent three months of money on a gym trainer and realized the terms of engagement were very different from the USA. There was no concept of postponing a session, and I ended up wasting many sessions when I traveled out of the city. I learned after being charged double that it's not more than ₹30 for a rickshaw to the metro station. I learned the trick of asking office janitors to do their job without offending them – by convening the message though the janitor's boss, the hand that pays his salary. I paid the price of waiting for friends. Then I learned that meeting friends at restaurants is about syncing their departure from their home and your departure from your home. What was intimidating and costly in the beginning was learnable in the end. It will help you be less afraid. Keep a buffer for the cost of settling down, because the quality of your life depends on one more thing – location.

Quality of Life in India Depends on Micro Location

My own experience can ascertain what Sameer Dixit, whom I introduced earlier, said, "Return to India is actually return to city." You can feel comfortable in one city and feel uncomfortable in another. Sameer would not have moved to India if he hadn't been able to move to the city his family lives in. Location matters.

However, micro-location matters more. Your choice of not just the city but also the exact location within that city matters a lot. Put together, these factors will determine the quality of your life in India.

The gods had blessed only one area of my Delhi apartment with a network signal. A conversation in any other part of the apartment sounded like, "So. rY? Ple rep ea t?" My experience of New Delhi was tinted red by the phone-throwing-feeling in areas where the network-sun didn't shine. When I moved within three months to a new rental apartment, the network issues vanished, but I had a new problem. Taxis would get lost in the look-alike lanes, and I'd be annoyed every morning explaining, "Bhaiiya, that main road is there no? Take left from main road and immediate right from second circle."

Your choice of not just the city, but also the exact location within that city matters a lot. Put together, these factors will determine the quality of your life in India.

Your experience of India will be clouded by the issues you face every day, adding to the *roz ki kich kich.*

You might miss out on opportunities too. If you ask me, "Does Pune have a running club? Did you join?" I'd say, "Yes, Pune has many running clubs, but I can't join them because of my location." My Pune home is in an old part of town – the trekkers club, writing meetups, and new restaurants are in the new part of town. Very far from my parents' home, making them inaccessible and affecting the quality of life I want to lead.

There is one factor that will add the biggest spark to your everyday life, and that is having friends or family in the same building. Not just nearby, no. In the same building. Within a distance that you can walk to in your pajamas.

In 2016, I was a freshly returned NRI in Bangalore and gladly moved in with a friend as her roommate. My roommate's office friends lived in the 4th-floor corner apartment above us. It was helpful having them around. I often left my keys with them, I borrowed their vacuum cleaner and hired their maid for our apartment. When the lights went out, they'd trot down the stairs, and we'd all be gathered on the couch, chattering around the dancing lights of a candle. There wasn't a hint of loneliness or second thoughts about life.

If you have to choose an apartment – prioritize being within pajama walking distance of a friend. Even if you don't like the apartment, you will love your life.

This is where India is so different from America – experiencing your community in that micro-location. It's the second-best thing after staying with family, which we talk about next.

Stay With Family or Not?

Manish Mehta, an NRI from Austin, was to move to his parents' home near Delhi, but he got an offer from a startup in Bangalore. He told himself, "You know what. Bangalore will do too." He decided excitedly to visit his parents at least once a month; no longer would he need to accumulate annual vacations to visit them or wish them on birthdays over video conference. He wouldn't need to suffocate over a 36-hour journey to get to them. Living independently and a short flight away from family worked for him. What could possibly go wrong?

When Manish moved to Bangalore, he found himself hesitating to book a flight to meet them, often abandoning his online cart. *Rs 10,000 for a 2-day visit to help Dad clean the water tank?* Manish would run the whole trip through his mind. *₹10,000, plus taxi, plus waking up early, plus airport anxiety… not worth it.* That year, his frequency to visit home was three times – for events that justified the spending – one for Diwali, one for Dad's milestone birthday, and another for an extra-long weekend.

Manish's story makes us understand the realities of living in a different city than parents.

If supporting your parents matters the most, live with them or close to them.

But living with parents can be difficult. Many NRIs wonder: *Will I get freedom to move around as I wish? Will parents still treat me like a child, telling me what to eat? Should I rent a home on the floor above them, or should I go to another city?*

I didn't think I would last very long staying at home with my parents. I was particularly skeptical about living with my dad because I am always fighting with him. Not the 'Give me your money' kind of fight that some homes have, but the 'Did you leave the light on?' kind of fight followed with 'No I didn't,' 'Yes you did,' 'No I didn't,' 'Yes you did.' As a school going kid, my grandmother, in her soft cotton sari, would ask me every day, "*Aavi gayi?* (You're home?)" At that age sarcasm was fun, and I'd say, "No, I'm still in school" and laugh at my own joke. I was afraid I would be asked these obvious questions by my parents. I was worried I'd have to live by their rules – Sleep by 10, wake at 6. I predicted that I was going to be bored, rebellious, and always irritated.

You can spend your life fearing the future, and the future turns out to be okay. My living with parents turned out to be much better than predicted. I still have 'You left the TV on' fights with my dad, but it is a source of entertainment.

There are still redundant questions. After I have a bath, Mom asks, "You had a bath?" but I seem to be okay with it. My heels announce my arrival from work, and I fling my purse on the couch and announce verbally, "I'm home!" My smile is wide, eagerly waiting for parents to ask me about my day, like my grandmother used to. I wish my grandmother were alive – I'd have run to her, knelt down, and put my head in her warm, welcoming lap, feeling the cotton sari against my cheeks and told her my stories, while she would have stroked my hair lovingly.

No family is the same. You might not have a great rapport with your family, or even if you do, you might be want to live independently. In this case, living close to your parents would be the best middle-ground approach.

The strange decision we NRIs have mentally made while living abroad is that we think our parents are immortal. You think your phone will always flash 'mom,' you think it's ok to surf the Internet when your father is on the phone with you, and you know they'll fly in to swing your newborn child in their arms. I am glad for the opportunity to know my parents as an older adult. The parents you know today are different from the parents you knew as you grew up. This makes the number one reason I will never regret moving home.

10

THE OFFICE

Your Temperament Decides How You Accept Work Culture

"I've heard horror stories from my friends about the work culture in India!"

– NRIs

It is fair that NRIs are worried about how they will adjust to work culture after so many years aboard. We've seen that your response to the work culture depends entirely on your temperament, environment, and luck. This whole chapter can be titled 'Your Mileage May Vary.'

I wonder how you are going to adjust to the work culture. What is your temperament like? Will your colleagues' sarcasm make you clench your teeth, or are you the type who would join him with a laugh and a 'back at you' rejoinder? Will you fill out HR's physical paper forms, shrug, and go back to your code, or will you figuratively slam the papers on your HR's desk and demand for making everything electronic and online? Will you be frustrated to stay up for an 11 PM meeting to suit someone's American time zone or will you do it willingly? Will you accept your founder's word for the product direction or will you publicly question your founders on it while others are quiet?

There are infinite directions your experience in a new work culture can be pulled into. Your success and happiness working in India vary *only* on the following parameters – your age, gender, temper, position, salary, number of people in your team, distance from your home, profile, coding language, street smarts – in short, your mileage may vary. Your feelings will vary on the many miracles that make you so uniquely you – the anger in your eyes, the voice modulation, or your positivity. Your friends' experience cannot be a predictor of how you will feel.

As much as I want to be unbiased, I have to say that working in India is genuinely more difficult than working in America. Work culture in India has been accused of many crimes – micro-management, unwritten policies that favor senior management, tight deadlines, bro culture, unprofessionalism. Someone could argue that every work-related issue Indians face is available in plenty in America.

Boss shouted at you? Happens in America too.

Boss took credit for your work? Happens in America too.

Boss gave you a fake deadline? Happens in America too.

I admit it does, but there are differences in work culture that are more prevalent and pronounced in India.

Allow me to show you what *really* changes in India.

What Is Really Different in Indian Work Culture?

Working in India Is Great Fun

Rohini Roy, a returned NRI from Philadelphia, is still chewing on the office canteen *saunf*, when she double taps the desk of her friend Maitri, who shoots up from her chair to join Rohini. They're going for their daily walk – two rounds of the Gurgaon office campus and a few rounds of discussions of the day.

Rohini tells me she loves this. She's made plenty of friends at work in India, sharing trivial frustrations or gentle gossip. She loves her breakfast buddies and her tea-time group; they meet every day. She never got to make this kind of a human connection in her 12 years of working abroad and finds this colleagues-become-friendly culture the best outcome of working in India. Her husband hasn't been so lucky. His office has a very young workforce that he's too senior to hang out with. He's been told, "Never a good idea to lunch with your team as they might stop taking you seriously." He follows that advice. It's a necessity that his office culture demands, and he doesn't question it.

The key difference between working in India vs. America is that the line between colleague and friend is fuzzy – your office colleagues *will* become your friends. Colleagues will ask you about your father's health, attend your wedding, and drop you home after a late-night beer Friday. Rohini loves this.

Additionally, Rohini feels, "If you are in your 20s, work life in India is like extended university. You will go to parties, outings, and movies after choosing friends from a large variety of people of your age group. If you are in your 30s, you will undoubtedly enjoy your colleagues' company, but it may be an uphill battle to find after-office hangout friends." People your age will probably have children and families to rush home to.

However, Rohini feels, for any age, office outings are way more fun in India than what she's seen abroad. She's splashed water with her team under a raging river waterfall. She's kicked a soccer ball in an office sports playoff. She's danced to a DJ's disk till late night in a top resort – a contrast with the ski and alcohol offsites she was used to in America.

Having worked in various places – government, on the ground, in a big company, and small startups – I have to concur. People are more friendly and personal. I haven't laughed so much in my life as I have with my co-workers in India. I look forward to the jokes untouched by political correctness and the ingenuity that people bring into conversations with you.

Still, India is full of contradictions and extremes. Working in India is fun for the same reason it is difficult – people are emotional, and they won't hide it. Let's talk about that next.

Indians Are Emotional

There is no way I can write this chapter without offending someone. Or without labeling Indians as 'they.' I am okay with you folding your arms across your chest and reading this – take it skeptically, or openly, or ignore it. Whatever you do, you have to understand that this section comes with a 'your mileage may vary' tag.

The average person in India is sensitive and emotional.

This means that when co-workers ask you how you are, they *really* want to know. The question 'How are you doing?' is not just a shallow greeting. There is empathy floating around. You have to hand this empathy back, though, and treat some people with caution. An example that stands out for me is my American-English emails offending someone. I have learned while dealing with traditional companies or traditional people (whatever that means) that it is advisable to start your requests with kindly. You want a stapler delivered to your desk? Replace 'I need a stapler' with 'I request you to kindly give me one stapler please.' Without the politeness-infused words, the sentence might look like an order to the reader and offend them. *Why is she ordering me? Who does she think she is? Coming in and telling me what to do!* Before you roll your eyes, I want to reiterate, this is for the traditional mindset only. The new generation companies won't give you this tickle.

There are two ways you can get work done at the office. The first way is by being the boss. There is another way – by being liked. If co-workers know you and like you, they will do favors for you, give you information, and help you when you're stuck. A friend narrated this incident to me: "My first week at the office in India, I would get lava red with anger. When I'd ask questions on an office women's WhatsApp group, no one would reply. Questions like 'Do you know a good tailor near office?' or 'Let's meet up for a walk' went unanswered. I felt stupid. This only got resolved after I showed up at lunch meets. The ladies got to put a face to a name, and the replies started coming in once they got familiar with me. Nothing replaces interaction."

Sensitivity makes giving feedback difficult as feedback may be taken personally. The average person wants to hear soft feedback, and any kind of direct feedback needs to be handled gingerly. Nickhil Jakatdar, an NRI who is the CEO of a Pune-based company, talks about how his senior managers are not able to give direct feedback. He says, "They put their feedback this way: Someone else told me that you're not performing, so I'm just conveying it. I don't feel that way. They do."

Everyone tries to be nice. Everyone wants to be liked. So Indians won't be too direct. And that's why you have to learn to take hints, like we saw in the 'You have to know' part of Chapter Nine. When someone says 'Yes, I'll call you soon,' it's just another way of saying No. A 'Yes, go ahead' might not mean the person actually agrees. They might be trying to be nice or non-confrontational. These subtle cultural nuances have to be picked up and learned for a happier life. This can only happen with time or with tips from close friends.

The need to be liked drives a fraction of co-workers to put in extra effort to make a boss feel liked. This is called *maska* (buttering up).

I once got critical feedback from a manager when I was leaving a project: "Nupur, you know what your problem is? You don't know how to put *maska. Tumhe maska lagana nahi aata* (you don't know how to butter up people). You think your work is going to do the speaking for you?"

This is the best feedback I've got. And the worst. The best because I tried – I am proud to say that I have actually googled 'How to put *maska*.' It's the worst feedback because I have not been able to ever implement it. I cannot pretend to like someone just because they are in a position of power.

Luckily, pandering to emotions that you're not comfortable with is not a necessary condition to do well at the workplace. You'll still do great if you have other skills. However, you might have some more problems in how people perceive you. Which we will talk about next.

NRIs Seen As Privileged

Eric Schmidt, the ex-CEO of Google, was immortalized in a meme after he spoke about a privilege. He said innocently during an all-hands: "...I have put these devices in my various houses...." It meme'd, because, you know, plenty of Californians can't afford even one home, and he had various houses! When Sheryl Sandburg (Facebook COO, born to wealthy parents) launched her book *Lean In*, critical feedback from her readers were of the form 'Of course you can lean in when you're born that rich!' Throughout the world, some people are treated by others as more privileged – even if they are humble about it.

Why is this important? In a typical Indian workplace, it is common to find people from diverse backgrounds, financial and cultural. There are some co-workers in India, who'll never have the privilege that NRIs are perceived to have – Money in dollars, that lilt to your accent, a wallet purchased from a Paris sidewalk hidden in the inner pocket of your purse, or running out of space on rapidly stamped passport pages. The international life is that of privilege, and you might be the privileged person in the eyes of some people.

This means that till the time you settle in at work, be careful about what you share. Voicing 'I went to New Zealand' with your hands tucked into your Northface jacket, might not be a great conversation to have with a new person.

Chinmayi Chavan, a recent ex-NRI who lived in Paris, had voiced during a team meeting a suggestion for improving the work culture. She tells me that she got sarcastic feedback from a man in her team. "Someone tell her this is India. Not her Europe." This is even while she was being humble and enthusiastic. If you shred humility and wear your NRI states with pride, telling people how you got a business class upgrade on the way to Hawaii or correcting your colleagues' pronunciation of schedule to skedule, you might make some silent enemies.

Throw cold water on this problem and share any privilege-sounding information only with someone who appreciates it. How do you know they will appreciate it? You won't. Take your time to figure that out. This is super difficult, because in the middle of crazy laughter at lunch, you might slip out to the whole group that "...I had bought these shoes when I was in San Francisco." People need time to get to know you, not in a suspicious sort of way, but in a gentle way. Use your judgment. Talking about time, here is the next problem – punctuality.

Punctuality Is an Issue

Another difference I've seen between working in America and India is the adherence to being on time. There is a pattern around being punctual in many cultures worldwide – for example, being late is okay in some cultures (like Italy or South America). Some countries are on military time (like Japan, Germany). In India, it's a mixed lottery. Different types of people have a different measure of time – some on time, some 10 minutes off, and some will leave their home after you have reached.

Throughout my life, I have been accused of being an on-time person. I've waited in wedding halls while the chairs are still being arranged. I've reached movie theaters before the previous movie was yet to end. I've stood in front of friends' doors and watched my clock at 7:59, so that I could knock at eight sharp. If there was a 'before-time peoples' meet-up group,' I would be the first to show up there too. This means I've always waited annoyed and alone, and perhaps, this makes me extra-sensitive to the topic of time-adherence.

In the workplace in India, I've discovered that hierarchy matters – you might always be in-waiting for the senior person. Co-workers who see you as a peer, might not bring the same sincerity to a meeting. I've waited 20 minutes in meeting rooms, with anger bubbling up inside me, sending 'I am in the meeting room' messages to colleagues. My anger would be extinguished with their sweet sorry. This waiting doesn't happen every time, but it happens often enough that I can say (with statistical significance) that your waiting time will increase in India. Except if you're the boss.

You might take time to adjust to the new punctuality and adjust you will. You might learn to meet serial offenders at their desk first to remind them about your meeting. For your friends, you might adjust your meeting place to one where you wouldn't mind waiting, like a bookstore. Or you might ask them to pick you up from your home. You will find a way to gauge if the 'I'll be there in five minutes' is really five or fifty minutes. Your time sensitivity will dull over time, making you a happier person.

You will learn to ignore unprofessionalism – or won't you? We dig into that next.

Unprofessional and Immature

In my survey of returned NRIs, I asked what problems NRIs faced while working in India. On top of the chart was 'Unprofessional and immature.' What does it mean?

You again will be reading this with folded arms. "Are you calling my Indian co-workers unprofessional, Nupur?" Of course not. There is a huge ***it depends*** tag to experiencing a work culture. There may be bias – for example, my experience doesn't match my sister's, who has worked in India for 20 years.

Many NRIs find that youngsters or fresh graduates are not equipped for the workforce in the same way a similar-age American would be. I agree with this looking at my own self. Look back at my early 20s, and I am horrified at the lack of awareness I had about conducting myself at work – giggling at a mistake, questioning without thinking, or giving feedback without facts. I'd never do that now.

After working 10 years in America, the contrast in what you could experience is high.

It was a winter afternoon in Bangalore, and in the little aisle near my office desk were standing three young men (or should I say, boys). I can still visualize them with their college backpacks and unpaid canteen credit. The three were physically interlocked – the tallest one was kicking shorty on his butt and the third boy wrapping his veiny hands around shorty's free arm. They were laughing, the type of laugh that if women did, would be called a giggle. So a male giggle.

I looked at them. They looked at me. What a sight – three giggling boys tickling and teasing each other in the middle of this MNC office. I stared at them, not understanding how to react. *Should I roll my eyes? Or should I wink at them, appreciating the fun they were having, like a fun colleague?* I thought more. *Would I see this in America? Three white boys kicking butt in office. Literally, kicking butts?*

Will this immaturity (or fun) affect your work? Maybe not. Will it affect your perception? Maybe.

A friend, who wishes to stay anonymous works at an MNC in Bangalore as a software engineer and narrates: "My manager occasionally refers to an older white-haired colleague as uncle. In his absence, of course. My team adds to these uncle jokes: 'Look at Uncle trying to write a document' just to stay in the manager's good books." After working for so long, I can recognize this judgmental behavior as unprofessional. I suspect some employees that report to such judgmental managers don't even know what they're doing.

The new generation is really getting better, but hierarchy is still a problem at the Indian workplace – we'll check that out next.

'Everyone Is Not Your Peer' Culture

Kavita Kanwal moved out of NJ after 12 years in America and found a job in Delhi as a manager – a team of 15 fresh graduates reported to her. Kavita treated everyone as her peer, as she used to in America. She was friendly, helpful, and often joked or chatted with her team. She recalls, "At the end of three months, when I'd get up from my chair, I knew a couple of funny guys were imitating my voice and gait behind my back. They stopped taking me seriously. In meetings, they'd WhatsApp chat under their desk. The only time they took me seriously was when I broke character and shouted at them." She adds, "But what can I do? They were professional in their work. They worked hard, worked overtime, and delivered the work. They also shied from asking me personal questions. I guess I really appreciate that." She shrugs when she completes her sentence.

Kavita is unhappy. She is used to treating everyone alike and finds that in India, she cannot afford to treat everyone equally. She has to be firm with juniors. She can't navigate this, and it eats into her every day at the office. She wonders how long she's going to last unless she changes. Will this happen to you? Who knows.

I personally had a sad experience. The friendly American question of 'Hey, How was your weekend?' was ingrained into my small talk. I used to 'How was your weekend?' everyone on Mondays. A senior manager in my India office took offense to my friendliness. He probably didn't want me to treat him like a peer and expected a distance from employees junior to him. I have since then substituted 'How was your weekend?' with a head nod, or just staring at the floor.

Some companies have a peer culture, and some don't. Traditional companies most certainly won't. If you like a peer culture, ensure you join a company that embodies it in its ethos.

Women at the Workplace

I can't help noticing that gender might affect the work opportunities you get. Men bond with each other over certain activities. If I were a young man, I'd be invited for a butt-kicking session with those three boys in my aisle. When stuck with a coding problem, they'd put their arms around my shoulder, and lean into my private space, and help me with my runtime error. They would know me better over 7 PM beers and later pull me into the future company they start. Would I get this opportunity while being a woman? Not so easily.

However, this is a global problem. I was in a Lean In session at the Google office in California, where a white lady told our group, "If I am 25% sad, my eyes are 100% sad. I cry very easily, but it doesn't mean I am not capable." She then narrated an incident of her director, a Caucasian female, who was so stressed out that she cried in front of a VP. "Now, the VP thinks my director is weak and not capable of handling people issues." **Perception of what a woman can or cannot do at the workplace is a global problem.**

In my personal experience, I suspect I am not taken too seriously by a specific type of people, because I am friendly and a woman. If I were a man with a deep voice, a no-nonsense look, and wore gray, ironed trousers, I would be taken seriously. A vendor I worked with couldn't believe I was the decision-maker and continued to ask, "Please connect me with your boss who will make the decisions."

Anindita Basu, an associate director of product management and consulting in the banking sector, has worked both in India and the US for more than 15 years. She flags a problem with diversity hiring. "You could be tagged and dismissed as a 'diversity hire.' People assume you got through only because you're a woman, even while you're completely loaded with skills, and you've earned your spot."

The women I interviewed for this book have not given much negative feedback about gender at the workplace. My advice is to assume all challenges for women in an American workplace are present in India.

Will You not Move Out of Fear?

This book has presented some irksome situations to you. Some might happen to you. Some might not. What if everything you fear is bound to come true? Will you not move to India out of fear?

You may be paralyzed by thinking of this future bad culture and choose to remain in inertia. An inertia that may produce boredom, depression, or longing – simply because you're afraid that someone in the future workplace may ask you about your divorce? Or because you're horrified from the tales of Anil's wife Sheila in Bangalore, who told you how her evil manager summons her back just when she's picked up her purse to leave for home? Or because a recently returned NRI is verbally abusing his life in India – "I am forced to attend 10 PM meetings with US clients!"

The fear of a bad work culture swings through my mind even today, but when I actually go to work, my fear takes a back seat. All the fear of 'what if I have a bad colleague' melts into the backbone of objectivity and experience. You will learn to deal with it too. Learn, adapt, and believe in learning from interaction.

> **All the fear of 'what if I have a bad colleague' melts into the backbone of objectivity and experience.**

I'll put forward some solutions on how to deal with your new work culture.

Dealing With the Change

Data analysis has a concept called A/B testing, where you keep attributes constant and change only one variable to see how the system responds to that change. With your move to India, many variables will change – your peers, physical space, commute time, personal relations, and manager. In this mix of spices, it's difficult to A/B test your feelings to find out why you're unhappy, or happy. You'll need to be very self-aware to pin-point which change is giving your soul pain or giving your soul happiness.

If there are so many changes in the work environment and culture, how does an NRI survive? We'll discuss how you may not just survive but thrive.

When Tejas Tyagi, a senior software engineer, switched jobs within the city of Seattle, he was finding fault at every small difference. I-520 increased his commute time by 18 minutes. His phone bill reimbursement wasn't automated. He'd complain to his wife, "Manager attached a 21-MB PowerPoint in his emails instead of using online slides! Who does that! I can't stand it." He compared and compared. His mind resisted the new culture, and eventually, he returned to his previous company on this side of Seattle.

When Tejas moved to India, he was skeptical about his happiness. He couldn't adjust to small changes in Seattle, how would he adjust in India?

But Tejas claims he was shocked to find himself not comparing even though his work life was significantly different. He was taking physical printouts for meeting clients, reminding staff to restock the coffee powder, and waiting without Internet in a room for five hours to meet a VIP – he didn't complain, compare, or cry. He felt fine. So what changed? What worked for Tejas?

Change Is so Large You Won't Notice the Small

The change from the US to India is of many magnitudes – it's difficult to compare. Even if you compare the difference, it might be harder to complain. You can't complain that you got blueberries for breakfast in the America office and not in India – blueberries aren't naturally available in India. It is very possible that you will completely dismiss differences in India that may look large from the American hilltop and go with whatever gets the work done.

Choose Better Work Content

If you like your work, you will survive. If you understand the importance of your work, you will not only survive, you will thrive. You might get better work in India, simply because of the freedom of choice. You can choose a different career because you're free from the handcuffs of visa restrictions (your own startup, your own business, or a non-conventional teaching job?). Also, because you may not need an immediate salary to pay the rent, you can take your time to find a job that suits you. This is for two reasons: One, most NRIs return to India with a decent buffer of savings. Second, rents in India eat a smaller percentage of your salary as the rents are more affordable. You can stay a few months in a rental place (or at a welcoming relative's place) without an income. This, in turn, showers ample time to search and evaluate a job you genuinely like. On a visa, you might have panicked into signing the first job that gets into your hand.

Being Around Family

I have corroborated an observation with singles – for single people, having family buzzing around presents a new meaning to work-life and a purpose bigger than yourself. Family is there to physically support you and mentally cushion you. There is much relief when you're digging your fingers into dal-rice after a long day, and you go, "Mom, remember that product manager I told you about? The one who only wears black t-shirts? He yelled at me during a meeting today!" Mom will put her chin on her palm and hear you vent it out. This local support changes your thinking – everything at work needn't be perfect anymore, and you don't feel alone in this office battlefield.

Be in a Position of Power

One way of dealing with the work environment in Indian culture is to be in a position of power. There are three sources of power: fame, money, and position. Assuming we are working-class, we may not be in control of fame and money. What we do have control over is to put ourselves in a position of power. This means, at the workplace, you could shamelessly be title heavy. You may need to scrap that 'code monkey' title you jokingly call yourself and instead be projected as Technical Director or Regional Manager. Even if it means you're opening tickets and collecting bug reports for management. It's a fine balance to be humble and be assertive at the same time, and that line is where you'll have to balance yourself.

I found this perceived power important – colleagues listen to you if you come backed with a title. Troublemaker co-workers will be on time for your meeting and will follow up on your requests. A veteran in the VC world told me that important people in traditional companies will not talk to people in other companies that are lower than a CXO title. In India, the title conveys impact and capability. Within their own company, a senior manager would talk to their managers in a formal way, while maintaining a certain distance commensurate with their seniority and position. I don't know why, but this is the way it is.

Don't Jump Right Into the Culture

It is the afternoon of a Monday in Oct 2016, in the Bangalore office, and I have little idea that this moment is going to change me forever.

I am about to make this monotonous meeting room a courtroom for the case of *Rude Man vs. Lady*. I think the man is rude specifically to this lady. He always cuts her off mid-speak. In California, you call it 'manterrupting,' which is simply a phrase for when a man interrupts a talking woman. California culture had coached me on how to deal with this manterrupting – Men interrupting women must be called out and discouraged. His behavior is completely unacceptable in California. Except that this is not California.

I take a whispered permission to call this impudence out from the lady who is sitting right next to me. Then I raise my hand and announce to the Manterruper, "You probably didn't mean it, but I just noticed you came across as being rude to her. Please allow her to continue to express herself." The Manterruper says 'sorry,' and the meeting moves on to the next topic of 'the API endpoints....' All acceptable outcomes of my calling him out.

The lady's reaction puzzles me. She ignores me. As if nothing has happened. She does not acknowledge my bravery. She does not put her hand on my shoulder. She does not say, "Thanks Nupur for helping me." I am surprised. I feel incredibly stupid for aggressively upholding a California rule in India and taking *panga* with the Manterruper, for a lady I know only for a few moons.

Months later, I was able to put the story together – the Manterruper and lady were friends, friends since 10 years. Their kids played together. Their spouses knew one another. That year, they wrote performance reviews for each other and it must have been bloody great because both got promoted. And me and my California justice package were left behind on the platform of the train called India, gaping in shock at what I'd done to make a fool of myself.

I realize now the lady did me a favor. The incident deepened my doubts about how prepared I am to 'take on' the navigational challenges of working in a different culture than I'm used to.

In India, you cannot assume the solutions in America are the same solutions for people in India. You cannot assume the priorities and preferences of people in America are the same in India. The only way to find out is to give yourself time. In your first six months in India, watch, and wait. If you act immediately, the outcome might not match what you are used to, and it could cost you anything – your face, your time, your reputation.

I have a clever aunt, who would always tell me: *"In sub jhamelo main mat pado,"* which meant, don't unnecessarily involve yourself in matters that might not concern you. There is to be a delicate balance – when do you decide it's time to help others, and when it's time to ask your inner morality police to sleep off?

I still stand up for my teammates, but I do it carefully. I haven't got over this incident fully yet, even after so many years. I hope you, dear reader, are braver than me.

What If You Are the Bad Culture?

David Dang was an admired team leader at Google. He was the perfect picture of Googliness – a radiating sweet smile, an appreciative leader (said 'Great idea!' often), and a storehouse of knowledge. I knew him well; he consumed my analysis reports and often consulted me on some topics.

David joined another large Silicon Valley company that presented the promise of making him an IPO millionaire. Years later, when I was wanting a change, I followed him there, looking forward to working in his organization. He looked the same – crew cut, fitting clothes with hands in the pocket. Except that I didn't recognize him. His eyes were restless, his smile was off, as if he was privy to something you didn't know. I saw what he did; he manipulated meetings to steer it back to his profit and approved requests that fit his agenda. *Was this the same David I knew?*

Same person, same job content but different company – it brought something else out of him. Was this his real personality? I think so. He decided to sober it down at Google – as many people do when they really want to adhere to the culture and not kick up a storm. The same person changed completely in a different environment.

Are you sure you're not David? You could be an angel in America and switch on your manipulation machine when you're working in India. We have seen many examples where NRIs 'behave' in foreign lands, but when they touch down in India, they become the very people they don't like. It could be possible that you might change your own attitude and become the person who is difficult to work with – watch out.

11

THE CONCLUSION

What to Do in Your Last Few Days in America

So have you decided to move to India?

If yes, I have a warning for you.

When you move to India, you could possibly be plagued by missing America terribly. Or maybe you will be okay. Or maybe not. Or maybe your spouse will miss America and get themselves to frequent trips, disrupting, at maximum, your life and, at a minimum, your schedule. We can't clearly predict if you will miss America or not.

But we can be better equipped to deal with it.

If you have decided to move to India, I want you to maximize your experience in the remaining time you have in America. As I've said before – squeeze the juice out of America. Remember, there are people all over the world that would be dying to be in your position – experiencing outdoors, learning new skills, and buying beautiful things. My recommendations are to do things that may not be in easy reach while in India.

1. America is the shopping druglord of today's material world. I have a mental list of things that I'll buy that when I visit America. All my electronics – headphones, keyboard, Mac, desk lamp, table lamp, music system, camera– have been bought frantically during my US visits. Buy it all there before you move!

2. Educate yourself. Join a weekend class. Better, join a certification course. Even better, get a degree.

3. Explore your city.

- Look up a travel guidebook of your own city in the local library. Visit all the places listed. While you're at the library, make a mental note to use the fantastic local library services often.
- Sign up for a walking tour of your own city.
- Make a hit list of restaurants and try them out, with company or alone! Bribe a friend with coffee or take a book with you.
- Schedule an activity for the weekday. Don't live your life just on weekends.

4. Travel and explore America
   - Mark dates on your calendar, and force yourself to take road trips every other weekend.
   - Make a list of the top ten cities you want to visit in America. Make it happen.

If you have decided to move to India, maximize your experience in the remaining time you have in America.

Write Your Own Chapter

Should you at least try to move to India? I think so. Though life is littered with examples of so many things I tried in life that fell through, yet when I look back, not doing it would have been wrong.

But you try only when it makes sense. Only when you *know* that moving is your answer. Don't try to move to India for the sake of moving to India. Don't try to move to India to keep a word you had given at a party or because you are the most patriotic in your group.

Don't allow fears to stop you – Fear of aunties, fear of salary decline, fear of missing out on crepes. An NRI once told me she had a fear that bridges will collapse in India. I would say, let the bridge collapse. Let the future loom on us like advancing gray clouds that know no fear themselves. Look at every change positively, and you'll face any gray clouds.

Failure is in non-action, when action is your answer. Stop waiting for things to happen to you. Live your life in America to the fullest, so that if you ever decide to leave, you will leave with satisfaction – that indeed, you have done the best you could.

Write your own chapter.

APPENDIX

EXERCISES

I have helped hundreds of NRIs through their fears of moving to India, to help them make a decision. I tell them to go through some of these exercises. Writing down your thoughts invites clarity and objectivity to your fears and feelings. So try the exercises below. It will help you spot the roadblock that your fear is feeding.

Exercise 1 - The Fear

Almost all NRIs I've helped in my consulting sessions have a lingering fear around them about moving to India. You probably do too. What fears do you have about moving to India? Write them here on the side of this page. Examples are:

- I fear the work environment
- I fear that I will not be able to find a job

After you've read the book, or if you already have, look at these fears with an objective eye. Are these simply worries and anxieties of an unborn future? Can you find a solution to each of these? How will you tackle or mitigate them in India?

Exercise 2 - Missing America

What do you think you will miss if you were to move? Write down all the small or big things you feel you will miss. For example, my list was:

✓ I will miss riding a bicycle on these smooth roads.

✓ I will miss hot water showers!

✓ I will miss the opportunities to travel the world.

Now compare this list with reality and the gravity of moving to India. Does it really hold up? Should it prevent you from moving? Prefix each line in your list with the words "I don't want to move to India because I am going to miss ___." This is how my list looks with that prefix:

- I don't want to move to India because I will miss riding a bicycle on smooth roads.
- I don't want to move to India because I will miss hot water showers!
- I don't want to move to India because I will miss the opportunities to travel the world.

Now read each line. Does it sound reasonable or stupid? Should I not move because I fear I am going to miss bicycle riding? Probably not. But the opportunities to travel might be legitimate.

× ~~I don't want to move to India because I will miss riding a bicycle.~~

× ~~I don't want to move to India because I will miss hot water showers!~~

✓ I don't want to move to India because I will miss the opportunities to travel the world.

Pick out sentences that check out to be legitimate. Find a friend to discuss it with. My fear of missing out on travel turned out to be invalid. I have traveled a fair bit since I moved, one of the many reasons was because I could use my vacation days for real vacations instead of exhausting them in India trips.

Exercise 3 - Take the Juice Out of America

This exercise is an extension of Chapter Eleven – it forces you to plan your next few years in America, whether you're ready to move or not.

What are the top things you want to explore while being in America? Write them down. For example, mine were:

- Visit Yellowstone National Park
- Travel to Seattle and Austin
- Join a professional photography course

Commit to exploring your list. Make a plan for the next six months. Definitely do it on the weekends but also plan for the weekday. Be specific and be proactive. For example, plan a trip to Miami. If you are looking for travel companions, plan it already and send the plan to your friends. When they see a plan, they will be more inclined to signup because you've done the hard work.

I hope these exercises help get you some clarity. Even if you see no immediate benefit, write out your answers. A few years later, when you brush past this book while adjusting your bookshelf and sorting your collection, you will turn the pages to your scribbled notes and smile. So much can change, and so much can be the same with time.

Made in United States
North Haven, CT
25 May 2022

19535100R00117